THE HAUNTER

GOOSEBUMPS®
Also available as ebooks

NIGHT OF THE LIVING DUMMY
DEEP TROUBLE
MONSTER BLOOD
THE HAUNTED MASK
ONE DAY AT HORRORLAND
THE CURSE OF THE MUMMY'S TOMB
BE CAREFUL WHAT YOU WISH FOR
SAY CHEESE AND DIE!
THE HORROR AT CAMP JELLYJAM
HOW I GOT MY SHRUNKEN HEAD
THE WEREWOLF OF FEVER SWAMP
A NIGHT IN TERROR TOWER
WELCOME TO DEAD HOUSE
WELCOME TO CAMP NIGHTMARE
GHOST BEACH
THE SCARECROW WALKS AT MIDNIGHT
YOU CAN'T SCARE ME!
RETURN OF THE MUMMY
REVENGE OF THE LAWN GNOMES
PHANTOM OF THE AUDITORIUM
VAMPIRE BREATH
STAY OUT OF THE BASEMENT
A SHOCKER ON SHOCK STREET
LET'S GET INVISIBLE!
NIGHT OF THE LIVING DUMMY 2
NIGHT OF THE LIVING DUMMY 3
THE ABOMINABLE SNOWMAN OF PASADENA
THE BLOB THAT ATE EVERYONE
THE GHOST NEXT DOOR
THE HAUNTED CAR
ATTACK OF THE GRAVEYARD GHOULS
PLEASE DON'T FEED THE VAMPIRE

ALSO AVAILABLE:
IT CAME FROM OHIO!: MY LIFE AS A WRITER by R.L. Stine

GOOSEBUMPS®

MOST WANTED
SPECIAL EDITION
THE HAUNTER

R.L. STINE

SCHOLASTIC INC.

Goosebumps book series created by Parachute Press, Inc.
Copyright © 2016 by Scholastic Inc.

ISBN 978-0-545-82545-0

10 9 8 7 6 5 4   16 17 18 19 20

Printed in the U.S.A.   40
First printing 2016

WELCOME. YOU ARE MOST WANTED.

Come in. I'm R.L. Stine. Welcome to the Goosebumps office.

Hey, you're just in time for lunch. Sit down at the table. I'm cooking up a hamster-and-cheese omelet. I know it sounds weird. But why waste a good hamster?

You don't want that? Okay. No problem. I have some leftover chicken lips I could warm up. They don't taste bad if you hold your nose while you swallow.

Whoa. You look a little sick. Let me get you something to drink. I have some delicious bat juice. You should try it. You know, it's very hard to squeeze the juice from a bat. They always put up such a fuss.

Well, okay, we can skip lunch. I see you are admiring the WANTED posters on the wall. Those posters show the creepiest, crawliest, grossest Goosebumps characters of all time.

1

They are the MOST WANTED characters from the MOST WANTED books.

That poster you are studying is of a creature called The Haunter.

Why do they call him The Haunter? Sammy Baker can tell you all about him. Sammy's story began on a dark, rainy Halloween night in an old haunted house. That's where Sammy ran into The Haunter. And that's where his nightmares started.

Go ahead. Read Sammy's story. You will soon find out why The Haunter is MOST WANTED.

PROLOGUE

I guess I could start my story by telling you about the school assembly on Monday morning. It will give you a good idea of what has been happening to me.

I pushed into the third row of the auditorium and dropped down beside my best friend, Bill Buzzner. (Everyone calls him Buzzy.) I had no idea that I was about to freak out and go totally wacko in front of the whole school.

My name is Sammy Baker. I'm twelve, and I never freak out or lose my cool or go berserk. I'm probably the quietest, nicest, most law-abiding, rule-following, do-good kid at Grover Cleveland Middle School. Ask anyone.

Even Miss Flake, my teacher, says I am the least trouble of any of her students. She says that's her highest compliment. Miss Flake says she would give me a gold star for attitude and a gold star for behavior. Except she doesn't believe in giving gold stars.

Miss Flake is very funny. She is always cracking jokes. She even makes fun of Mr. Harkness, the principal. She croaks in a deep, booming voice and struts around with her eyes popped out until she almost looks like a big frog. Just like Mr. Harkness. It always makes us roar.

She tells everyone that she has been a Flake her whole life.

I like a teacher with a good sense of humor—don't you? I don't even mind all the homework she gives us—at least two hours a night.

But today I wasn't laughing. We were supposed to go on a field trip to a farm where they make maple syrup. I mean, where they tap the trees and collect the syrup in buckets. Then we were all supposed to get a big pancake lunch with real maple syrup.

But the trip had to be canceled because Mr. Harkness decided to invite Mayor Springfield to school for an assembly about city government.

City government? Big whoop, right?

No field trip. No pancakes. And a boring lecture.

As we took our seats in the auditorium, I wanted to complain to Buzzy about how unfair it was. But he was talking to Summer Magee, who sat on his other side.

I couldn't blame him for ignoring me. Summer is one of the hottest girls in school. I've had a mad crush on her since third grade, when we built a volcano together for the science fair.

Summer saved my life when the volcano exploded and a wave of burning hot lava gushed onto the front of my T-shirt. She grabbed the shirt in both hands—and ripped it off my body before I was too badly burned. The class went wild.

I've had a thing for her ever since.

But let's face facts. In the past three years, Summer hasn't paid much attention to me at all. I think maybe she was disappointed that our volcano was such a loser. Or maybe she doesn't even remember the whole thing.

Summer has wavy blond hair, dimples in both cheeks, sky-blue eyes, and an awesome smile. She is the star of the gymnastics team. She is small and light and amazing on the balance beam. And why am I going on and on about her?

I guess because she was telling some kind of long story to Buzzy and ignoring me as usual.

The auditorium was nearly full. The roar of voices echoed off the dark walls as we waited for the presentation to begin. Mr. Harkness was already onstage with the mayor. They were both standing behind the podium with their arms crossed in front of them, wearing identical brown suits.

As I said, Mr. Harkness looks a lot like a very big frog. Mayor Springfield is tall and skinny and kind of hunched over and makes me think of a praying mantis. His glasses catch the light, so you can't see his eyes.

I turned and saw my archenemy Rubin Rubino squeezing into my row. Rubin tripped over a kid's shoes and bumped a girl sitting in the row in front of us. As he started to edge past me, he stomped down hard on my right sneaker.

Pain shot up my foot and leg and I let out a shriek.

"Oops. Sorry," Rubin said. He flashed me that grin with his two front teeth poking out, and his big black eyes laughing, always laughing.

Rubin loves to cause me pain. He's big and he's strong. He's built like a wide-body truck. He has thick, clumpy black hair that sticks out all over his round, pudgy head and makes him look like a caveman.

Rubin always appears to be laughing or grinning or smiling or chuckling. I don't think I've ever seen a serious expression on his face. Even when he's dishing out the hurts.

Why does he love to pick on me and make my life a world of pain?

Well, last year, he was showing off in front of a group of high school girls, telling them how great he is on a skateboard. And I came along and accidentally tripped him. His board went flying, and he fell on his face on the sidewalk and got a bloody nose.

The girls all thought it was a riot. And they laughed their heads off.

That's why he has been my archenemy ever since.

Rubin mussed up my hair as he squeezed down the aisle. He dropped heavily into the seat next to Summer. He took Summer's face in both of his big hands and turned her head so she was facing him and not Buzzy. Then Rubin started talking to her.

Buzzy had no choice. He turned to me. "What's up, Sammy?"

I shrugged. "I'm just bummed that our field trip was canceled."

Buzzy frowned at me. "But you don't like maple syrup."

"I know," I said, "but I like getting out of school and just hanging out someplace."

Buzzy and I look a lot like brothers. We both have short, light-brown hair and brown eyes. We're about the same size, average in every way, not too tall or short, not heavy or skinny.

If you describe Buzzy, you pretty much describe me. Except I'm quieter than he is. His parents call him Motor Mouth. He talks a lot and gets more excited about things than I do.

And Buzzy is braver than me. I admit it. I try hard not to be a wimp. But lots of things creep me out.

Buzzy had his eyes on the podium onstage.

"We had to listen to Mayor Springfield talk in my old school," he said. "Do you know what he invented?"

I shook my head. "No. What did he invent?"

"He invented *boring*."

We both laughed. The auditorium lights dimmed. Onstage, Mr. Harkness cleared his throat into the podium microphone. A deafening squeal from the loudspeakers made everyone scream.

"Sorry about that," the principal croaked in his froggy voice. He cleared his throat again. "I'm proud to introduce our special guest this morning. As many of you know, Jonathan Springfield is the mayor of our town. And he has come to give you all a special inside look at how city government works."

Some kid near the back of the auditorium yawned really loud. That made a lot of kids laugh.

Mr. Harkness waited till everyone calmed down. "This is a special opportunity for us," he said. "And I want you all to show Mayor Springfield our best Grover Cleveland Middle School behavior."

The loudspeaker squealed again. "Let's all give the mayor a round of applause," Mr. Harkness said.

Kids clapped and I heard some sarcastic cheers. I saw Katie Springfield, the mayor's daughter, a seventh grader, sitting at the end of the first row. She had her head down and looked totally embarrassed. I felt bad for her. I mean, who wants their father to come to school?

The mayor pulled some papers from his jacket pocket. His speech. He lowered his skinny praying-mantis head toward the podium and began to read. He had a soft voice and spoke in a low drone. I could barely hear him.

I waited, half-listening for about ten minutes. Then I jumped to my feet. Stepping over shoes, I began to push my way to the aisle.

"Hey, Sammy. Sammy—where are you going?" Buzzy called to me in a loud whisper.

But I ignored him. I stepped into the aisle and began to walk toward the stage.

You'll probably be a little surprised by what I did. I know I was very surprised myself.

You see, I climbed onstage and walked up beside the mayor. And then I did a wild, crazy tap dance in front of the whole school. And as I did my nutty tap dance, I flapped my arms in the air and crowed at the top of my lungs like a rooster.

I had to do it. I had no choice. I couldn't help myself.

Why?

It's kind of a long, scary story. . . .

PART ONE

3 WEEKS EARLIER

Halloween was less than two weeks away, and I have to admit, it's not my favorite holiday.

I try hard not to be a wimp or a scaredy-cat. But the truth is, I've never seen the fun part of people scaring each other.

Buzzy loves scary movies and books, but not me. I don't like that feeling of being frightened, that tingling at the back of my neck, or that cold feeling rolling down my body, or suddenly getting clammy, wet hands, or that gasping surprise that makes me want to scream.

Scary stuff isn't fun.

Thinking that someone is lurking in your bedroom closet or hiding in the dark basement waiting to pounce isn't fun. Or that the living dead are staggering toward you, craving your flesh, or that a vampire is going to grab you in the night and sink his teeth into your throat.

How can those things be fun?

I know, I know. A lot of people don't agree

with me. Buzzy calls me a chicken and a coward and a wimp when we're hanging out and he wants to pick a scary movie to watch on Netflix. And maybe he's a little bit right.

But there's no law that says you *have* to like being scared—is there?

When Buzzy asked me what I wanted to be for Halloween, I just stared at him. "Buzzy, we're twelve," I said. "We're too old to go trick-or-treating. It's for little kids."

He called me a jerk. Then he called me a coward and a chicken and a wimp. *And that kid is my best friend!*

It's always cold and dark and creepy on Halloween night. And there are people out all over the neighborhood waiting to scare you and make you jump or scream.

Why do I need that? I'm plenty scared of real-life things. Like getting a D in Algebra. Or dropping my lunchroom tray in front of Summer Magee and all the cool kids. Or Rubin Rubino— mainly because even a whole year after the skateboard accident, he still loves to torture me and pick on me and embarrass me and hurt me. And always with that toothy caveman grin on his face and those eyes that always seem to be laughing.

And that's why I was about to have the worst Halloween of my life. The worst night of my life. And the most terrifying time I ever had.

And it was all Miss Flake's fault.

Miss Flake loves Halloween. No big surprise. She has a picture of Count Dracula hanging on our classroom wall next to a painting of George Washington.

One day, Misty Rogers, a girl in our class, asked Miss Flake why that picture was up there. And Miss Flake replied, "It's just a reminder."

A reminder of *what*?

Miss Flake didn't say.

But there it was, that dark photograph taken from the original *Dracula* movie staring down at us with the vampire's eyes gleaming and his fangs about to slide down over his lips.

A reminder.

That day, Miss Flake wore a bright green sweater over faded jeans. Her light brown hair was tied behind her head in a ponytail. She had long, dangly plastic earrings in her ears. She's young and pretty and nice—and she was about to ruin my life.

She sat down on the edge of her desk and crossed her legs in front of her. "Halloween is almost here," she said. "I know you all love Halloween as much as I do."

I had an urge to raise my hand and say I didn't love it. But how uncool would that be? I glanced at Summer Magee sitting right in front of the teacher in the first row. I never wanted to look uncool in front of Summer.

17

"So I have a special Halloween research assignment for you," Miss Flake continued. "I'm going to divide the class into four groups. Each group is going to study a different topic."

She pulled up some papers from her desk. She lowered her voice: "These topics are *verrrrry sssscaaaary*," she hissed like a movie vampire. "I hope you don't get nightmares."

Hope I don't, I thought. What kind of research paper could be so scary?

"Here are the four topics we are going to explore," Miss Flake said. She read from her paper: "One. *Vampires—Fact or Fiction?*"

Some kids giggled. "I want that one!" Buzzy called out.

Miss Flake shook her head. "No, you don't get to pick. I've already divided you up into groups." A few kids groaned.

She raised the paper. "Now let me finish. This is going to be fun. The other three topics are: *The History of Graveyards*; *Magic Spells and Legends About Witches*; and *Are Haunted Houses Real?*"

Everyone started talking at once. Kids were shouting out which topics they wanted. Rubin Rubino cupped his hands around his mouth and began making spooky ghost sounds. *"Owooooo owoooooo."*

I stayed silent. I was thinking hard, wondering which group Miss Flake had put me in. I hoped it wasn't the haunted house group. I have a thing about haunted houses.

Once, Buzzy forced me to watch that *Ghost Hunters* show on TV. I watched those guys go into an old house and capture eerie sounds and shadows that couldn't be explained. I mean, the only explanation was that ghosts are *real*. And I sure didn't want to believe that.

There's an abandoned house in our town everyone calls the Marple House. And everyone in town believes it's haunted. I don't believe in ghosts. But when I pass the Marple House, I always ride my bike on the other side of the street. I mean, why take chances?

Miss Flake had a big stack of papers in her hand. She walked down the aisles between our seats, passing them out. "These are your group assignments," she said. "I tried to give you each a topic you will be interested in."

Please, no haunted house, I thought. I crossed my fingers on both hands. *Please, no haunted house.*

Miss Flake handed me my assignment paper. I raised it to my face, read the words at the top, and gasped. My assignment: *Are Haunted Houses Real?* Those four words were about to ruin my life.

"It's awesome that we're in the same study group," Buzzy said.

I didn't reply.

It was a few hours later, and Buzzy and I were walking home after school. It was a gray October day. A cold breeze chilled my face, and dark clouds rolled low over the sky. Perfect weather for the dark mood I was in.

"Yeah, I guess it's good," I mumbled finally. "But I don't want to be in this group. I don't want to study haunted houses. No way."

Buzzy chuckled. "Same old Sammy."

I shivered, not from fear but from the cold wind. "It's not like I'm afraid," I said.

"Of course not. You? Afraid?" Buzzy said. I knew he was making fun of me.

"I'm just not interested in ghosts," I said. "I think they're totally boring."

Buzzy chuckled again. His chuckling was starting to annoy me.

We crossed the street and followed the path into Washington Irving Park. A gust of wind made all the trees creak and bend. Dead leaves came raining down all around us. Our houses were on Fairmont Street, on the other side of the park.

"So you wouldn't be frightened to spend Halloween night in a haunted house, searching for ghosts?" Buzzy asked.

I shivered again. From the cold. "I'd just be bored," I said.

Okay, okay. I'm a liar. Sue me.

I pulled off a crackly brown leaf that clung to my wool cap. I kicked a white pebble off the dirt path. Just because I felt like kicking something.

"Studying a haunted house isn't the worst part," I told Buzzy.

He stopped walking and turned to me. His gray hoodie was pulled up tight around his face. His cheeks were red from the cold. "What's the worst part?"

"Rubin Rubino," I said. "Why does he have to be in our group?"

Buzzy shrugged. "Miss Flake probably doesn't know Rubin uses you as a punching bag."

I shook my head. "When he looks at me, he sees a big black-and-white target painted on my face."

Buzzy clapped me on the shoulder. "Know what? I'll bet you could take Rubin in a fight."

I pulled away from him. "Are you kidding me? He's twice my size. His arms are fatter than my legs! Rubin couldn't play on the softball team because they couldn't find a glove big enough to fit his hand!"

"Maybe there's some place you could go and take fight lessons," Buzzy said. "You know. Like karate or something. You could learn how to kill people with your bare hands . . ."

I stared at him. "You're serious?"

He shook his head. "Just saying."

Buzzy is a good friend. But sometimes he has weird ideas.

"I don't want to be in the same study group with Rubin," I repeated.

"But we could have fun," Buzzy said. "I have this cool idea. We collect a lot of ghost-hunting gear and we go to Marple House on Halloween night. Everyone knows the house is haunted, right? We spend Halloween night inside it and test the place for ghosts. It could be awesome."

"Not awesome," I said. "Definitely not awesome." I tugged my red wool ski cap down over my ears. "Stay up all night on Halloween in a haunted house? I won't come. I'll say I'm sick or something. I won't go in that house on Halloween night—especially with Rubin Rubino there. He'll do everything he can to scare me. He'll—"

"But Summer Magee is in our group, too," Buzzy interrupted.

My mouth dropped open. I had stared so hard at Rubin's name on our group list, I hadn't read any of the other names.

"Summer?" My mind began to spin. It was a chance to impress her. To show her how brave I was in the face of the supernatural. Maybe save her life the way she saved mine.

Whoa. Who was I kidding? The whole idea of spending Halloween night in Marple House terrified me. But with Summer in our group, I had no choice. I had to show up.

After school the next day, I looked for Buzzy but I couldn't find him. I took a deep breath, adjusted the backpack over my coat, stepped out of the school building, and headed toward Rubin Rubino's house.

Everyone liked Buzzy's idea about Marple House, so we were meeting at Rubin's house to make a plan. As I headed over there, I had a heavy feeling in my stomach, as if I'd swallowed a bowling ball.

It was a sunny afternoon but cold. The nearly bare trees cast long shadows over the sidewalk.

Rubin lives three blocks from school, on the far side of Washington Irving Park. This is the neighborhood of big, expensive houses with wide front yards and tall hedges.

Walking this way meant that I had to pass Marple House. Now I had *two* bowling balls in my stomach. Of course, I stayed on the other side of the street. But even on such a bright,

24

sunlit day, the big old house hunched in shadow. The shingles were blackened as if they had burned in a fire. Several windows were missing their glass. The screens over the front porch had been missing for as long as I could remember.

The air seemed to grow colder as I stopped to stare. I shielded my eyes with one hand and gazed up to the top of the tall house. A flash of light in an upstairs window caught my eyes.

No! A pale face peering down. Someone in the window. Someone watching me.

Impossible.

I blinked a few times. Looked away. Looked back up.

It was gone.

The sunlight had played a trick on me. My heart was pounding hard. I scolded myself for having too good an imagination.

It *was* just my imagination, I told myself.

The windows were all as dark as the blackened shingles now. I waited a few seconds to catch my breath. Then I turned and took off. I ran the rest of the way to Rubin's house, my backpack bouncing hard on my back.

The face in the window lingered in my mind. No. Not a face. Just a patch of sunlight. That's all.

I ran the whole two blocks to Rubin's house. It was a huge redbrick house with a wide front yard that stretched forever. A high evergreen hedge blocked the view of the house from the street.

I started walking up the long gravel driveway that stretched between a gap in the hedge. Up ahead, I could see Rubin's four-car garage.

Marple House was big. But this house was like a mansion. It even had *two* front doors.

I knew his parents were rich. Rubin brags about it a lot. His mother is a chemist. And she got rich by inventing some new kind of acid.

I rang the brass doorbell on the first front door I came to. After a few seconds, the door swung open, and a young woman in a gray-and-white maid's uniform greeted me. "Your friends are all downstairs," she said.

She led me to a stairway at the end of a long hall. As I walked, I glimpsed an enormous living room to the left filled with dark, heavy-looking furniture and a dining room to the right with a crystal chandelier hanging over a table that appeared to be a mile long.

I heard voices as I made my way down the carpeted stairs. "Hey, Sammy. There you are!" Buzzy cried as I stepped into a playroom.

I blinked as my eyes adjusted to the bright lights. The walls were striped, yellow and red. The chairs were all crazy bright colors, too. The room looked like it belonged in some kind of carnival.

I saw a foosball table and an air hockey game

in the center of the room. Against the wall, Shamequa Shannon and Todd Garcia were bending over a *Simpsons* pinball machine, making it clang *bing bing bing*. Summer Magee sat on a purple couch, a slice of pizza on a plate in front of her.

Rubin appeared from another room, carrying a handful of Cokes. He set them down on the table beside the pizza box and grinned at me. "Hey, Sammy."

"Hey," I murmured. I'd never been to Rubin's house. I mean, he wasn't exactly a friend. And I was having a lot of trouble taking this room in. It was pretty awesome.

Buzzy opened a can of Coke and gulped it down. "Guess we're all here," he told Rubin. He dropped into a rubbery pink chair.

Rubin tried to push down his hair with both hands. It bounced right back up. He grinned at me again. "How's it going, Sammy?"

"Okay," I murmured. I don't like it when Rubin pretends to be friendly.

An explosion of sound came from the pinball machine. Shamequa and Todd both cheered and slapped high fives.

Shamequa is tall and very pretty, with brown skin and straight black hair pulled back in a long ponytail. She's very quiet and a little bit shy. She wore a white sweater pulled down over a short black leather skirt, over black tights.

27

Todd is the class clown. I mean, he's always goofing on everything. He has spiky white-blond hair, weird pale gray eyes, and a scarecrow body. He really looks like a stick drawing, even though he eats more than anybody.

He's always tumbling and bouncing off walls and deliberately walking into people. It's like he never stops. He just loves cracking everyone up.

Summer Magee turned, seeing me for the first time, and her eyes widened in surprise. "Sammy? I didn't think you'd come," she said.

I walked over to the purple couch. "Hey, I'm into this," I lied. "We got the best assignment."

Her eyes studied me. Could she tell I was lying? Could she tell I'd almost chickened out and went home instead of coming here?

"I didn't think you liked ghosts and supernatural stuff," she said.

"Who—me?" My voice cracked. I guess I got excited because Summer actually noticed me. "I'm totally into science," I said. "And what we're going to do . . . It's an awesome science experiment."

She stared at me.

Why did I always sound so awkward when I talked to her?

I'm totally into science? How could I say such a stupid thing?

"Let's get started," Rubin said. "Better grab some pizza. Only three slices left."

Shamequa opened the box and lifted out a slice. Todd dropped down on the purple couch and sat in Summer's lap. She cried out in protest and shoved him off with both hands. He pretended to fall off the couch, then sat cross-legged on the floor.

Summer rolled her eyes. "Very mature, Todd," she said. "I mean really." She shoved the back of his neck.

Todd didn't care. He pretty much does whatever he feels like, and he doesn't care what people think of him. When we're in the haunted house, Todd will probably just crack jokes or fall down the stairs to get laughs or do something nutty, and he'll scare away the ghosts.

Shamequa is like the opposite of Todd. She hardly ever speaks. When she does talk, she has this tiny voice that's no louder than a whisper. She has three little sisters, and sometimes I help her take care of them after school.

To my surprise, Rubin walked over and took me by the arm. I started to pull back. I knew what he was planning—to twist my arm and make me scream.

But no. He guided me past the long coffee table to a yellow chair across from Summer and Todd. "I saved this chair for you, Sammy," he said. He had pizza sauce on his chin.

I was too surprised to say anything. Why had he saved a chair for me?

I found out as soon as I sat down on it. After a few seconds, I felt something warm soak through my jeans. Something warm and wet.

"Whoa." I jumped to my feet. My butt and the back of my jeans were soaked. I rubbed my hand over the wet spot. It smelled bitter.

"Rubin—what *is* that?" I cried. "What did you *do* to me?"

His eyes flashed. "Is it starting to burn? I wanted to test out my mom's new acid. Count to ten, Sammy. In ten seconds, your jeans are going to disintegrate. HA-HA-HA. You'll be naked!"

5

I let out a shriek. "Acid? Really?"

Shamequa and Todd leaped to their feet, their eyes wide with alarm. Summer screamed. "Rubin—you *didn't*!"

Rubin shook his head. "No, I didn't. Of course not. It's not acid, Sammy. I was just messing with you."

"Then . . . what *is* it?" I realized my legs were trembling. "What *is* it?"

Rubin shrugged. "Calm down, okay? My cat had an accident before everyone showed up."

I shrieked again. "Your *what*? Your cat peed in the chair?"

He grinned that toothy grin at me. "That's why I saved that chair for you."

Summer narrowed her eyes at Rubin. "You have an evil mind," she said. "That's *sick*."

His grin grew wider. "I know."

"You went too far," Shamequa scolded him. "You scared poor Sammy to death."

"No, he didn't," I said quickly. "I wasn't scared at all. Just a little . . . surprised."

"Why are you always picking on Sammy?" Buzzy asked him.

Rubin laughed. "He knows why. Okay, sit down, guys." He motioned with both hands. "We've had our fun time."

Fun time? That's what he calls fun time?

"Let's get down to business," Rubin said.

Shamequa and Todd dropped back onto the couch. Standing there in the wet jeans, I didn't know what to do or where to go. *Awkward.* My legs felt sticky. I couldn't shut out the sharp, sour smell.

What should I do? Just go home?

No. That's what Rubin wanted. Holding my breath from the sick odor, I sat back down in the chair.

Rubin grabbed the last pizza slice from the box. Then he draped himself over the arm of the red chair across from me. "It's your genius idea, Buzzy," he said. "Why don't you explain it to everyone."

Buzzy explained his idea. "We get a bunch of ghost-hunting equipment . . . EMF meter, full-spectrum cam, EVP recorder . . . We go to Marple House on Halloween night. We stay there all night collecting proof that the house is haunted. The next week, we present our report to Miss Flake, and we all get As."

I felt a chill at the back of my neck. Buzzy made it sound so simple. But he left out one important detail. We were trying to find a ghost. What if there really *was* a ghost in Marple House? Ghosts aren't always friendly. If ghosts were friendly, there wouldn't be so many terrifying ghost stories.

I squirmed in the chair, my legs still sticky inside the wet jeans. Was I the only one who thought about this? I decided not to say anything. I didn't want to be the first to sound scared.

Todd tilted a Coke can to his mouth and took a long drink. He crushed the can in his hand and heaved it at Buzzy. "How do we know Marple House is really haunted?" he said. Then he burped loudly for nearly a minute.

"Everyone knows it's haunted," Buzzy said. "I only moved here two years ago, and the first thing I learned about this town was that Marple House is haunted."

"It's haunted by the ghost of a boy, right?" Summer said. "People who live on that block hear him screaming late at night?"

I hoped no one in the room saw me shiver. If the ghost boy screamed a lot at night, he probably didn't want company.

"I heard he was hit by a lightning bolt," Todd said. "ZZZZZZZAP!" He swung his hand down hard and smacked the chair arm. "It was a big thunderstorm. The lightning burned him up totally. His family was away. When they got home, they couldn't find him. He had completely burned to nothing."

"No ashes?" Shamequa said.

Todd shook his head. "His ashes burned, too."

"They never found a trace of him," Buzzy said. "The family was so heartbroken, they moved to another town as fast as they could. They didn't realize they were leaving his ghost behind. The boy's ghost has been trapped in the house ever since. And late at night, he screams for his parents . . . who never come."

I made a gulping sound. I didn't mean to. It just slipped out from my throat.

When I looked up, everyone was staring at me. "Are you too scared to do this?" Rubin asked.

"Scared? No way," I said. "I think it's an awesome plan. I love it. It's going to be the most amazing Halloween ever. I can't wait. I'll go in first if you want me to."

I gazed at Summer. Was she buying my lies? Did she believe me?

No way I'm going to show up on Halloween night, I told myself. *What if the ghost boy wants revenge or something? What if he locks us in the house and . . . and . . .*

I didn't want to think about it. I just knew I would not be joining this group for a night in the haunted house.

Everyone was still staring at me. Luckily, there was a voice in the stairwell, followed by footsteps, and they all turned to see who was coming down.

Misty Rogers appeared, breathing hard, her hair wild around her face, her cheeks red. "Sorry I'm late," she said, trying to smooth down her tangles of wavy black hair with both hands.

We all laughed. You see, Misty is always late for everything. And she never has a good reason. She just runs on a slower clock than the rest of the world.

"What did I miss?" she asked, pulling off her coat and tossing it over the air-hockey table. She wore a red sweatshirt over faded jeans.

"Everything," Summer told her.

Misty lifted the lid on the empty pizza box and peered inside. "I see I missed the pizza, too." She lowered herself to the floor and leaned her back against the coffee table. "I heard we're going ghost hunting."

"We're going to prove there's a ghost in Marple House," Buzzy said. "And we're all going to get As."

Misty scrunched up her face. "*Ewww.* What's that smell?"

"It's Sammy," Rubin said. "He had an accident."

Misty squinted at me, holding her nose.

"I did not!" I cried. "It was Rubin's cat!"

"My dad has a lot of professional ghost-detecting equipment I can borrow," Shamequa said. "I know he has an EMF meter and a portable motion sensor. And I think he has a remote digital thermometer we can use to see when the ghost makes the room temperature go down."

"That's awesome," Buzzy said. "Is he really into ghost hunting?"

"He was for about ten minutes," Shamequa replied. "Then he switched to UFOs. The ghost-hunting equipment just sits in a closet."

"Perfect," Rubin said. "How cool is this? We won't even have to make our own equipment."

Everyone started talking at once. They were all totally excited about Buzzy's haunted house idea. My mind was spinning. I was trying to decide which excuse I would use to get out of going with them on Halloween night.

Should I come down with the flu or some mysterious illness? Should I have to visit my cousins in another city? Should I say my parents needed me to help clean the basement? Which excuse would everyone believe?

I was still trying out excuses in my mind when the meeting broke up. It was nearly dinnertime. We all stampeded up the stairs. I couldn't wait to get home and get out of these smelly cat-pee jeans.

Summer stepped up beside me as I made my way down the gravel driveway to the street.

"Rubin is so mean to you," she said. "He's really awful."

"He was absent the week we had that unit about bullying," I said. "He thinks it's still cool."

I was kind of making a joke, but she didn't laugh. We stopped at the bottom of the driveway. "Are you really going to come Halloween night?" she asked. "You know Rubin will probably do something horrible to scare you to death."

I shrugged. "I can handle Rubin."

Her eyes studied me. I stared back at her. "I'll be there Halloween night," I said. "No way I'd miss it. We'll see who's brave and who isn't."

She nodded. I still couldn't tell if she believed me or not.

A cold breeze shook the trees. I zipped my coat to the top, then shoved my hands into the pockets.

"Well. Bye," she said. The longest conversation we'd had in three years.

We headed off in different directions.

That night was when the nightmares began.

That night I dreamed I was inside Marple House. I stood in a bare room of dark wood floors and olive-green walls. No furniture. It was daytime. A slender beam of sunlight washed in through a single dust-smeared window.

And a boy stood stiffly in front of the window, his face hidden in shadow. I was standing close enough to reach out and touch him. He took a step out of the shadow, and I could see his empty eye sockets. His eyes were missing. Under the deep holes in his face, his mouth twisted in a menacing scowl.

I turned away. I couldn't bear to look at him. Wave after wave of panic rolled down my body. I shut my eyes and wished myself out of there.

I knew I was dreaming. I struggled to raise myself, to pull myself up from the ugly dream, away from the boy with no eyes.

But no. When I turned back, I was still in that narrow room, still standing across from the scowling boy. Trapped in the dream. Unable to escape it.

And then the boy stuck his arms straight out, as if reaching for me. He staggered toward me. Closer . . . closer . . .

I woke up.

I woke up drenched in sweat. I blinked myself awake. Struggled to force the terrifying picture of the eyeless ghost boy from my mind. My hands ached from squeezing the bedsheets so tightly. My throat felt raw and sore. Had I been screaming?

I stood up and stretched my hands above my head. I took a deep breath.

"Only a dream," I murmured out loud. "It was only a dream."

But I knew one thing for sure. I was not going to spend Halloween night in Marple House. No way. The dream was a warning. And I always listen to warnings.

I dropped back onto the edge of my bed. I knew what I had to do.

I had to tell Mom and Dad about this scheme. I had to tell them the plan to go ghost hunting all night in that old, abandoned house.

No way they would ever let me do it.

Too dangerous. Too frightening. My parents know me. They know it wouldn't be good for me. They know how much I would hate staying in the house. They know how scared I would be.

I should have realized right from the beginning. My parents would save me. My parents would give me the excuse I needed not to go through with this horrible plan.

I felt better already. I settled back on my bed. I couldn't get to sleep, but I didn't care. My worries were over.

At breakfast, I told Mom and Dad about the overnight ghost hunt.

"Do you believe they want to stay all night in Marple House?" I said. "No parents. No one there to watch over us . . . All night in that freezing-cold abandoned house. Can you believe that?"

Mom stared across the table at me. Dad lowered his coffee mug. They exchanged glances.

"That's wonderful!" Mom exclaimed.

A smile spread over Dad's face. He usually never smiles in the morning. He hates mornings. "Great idea," he said.

"I'm proud of you, Sammy," Mom said. "Proud that you want to do something so brave. We know how frightened you are at Halloween time. Time to get over those silly fears."

"Well . . ." I started.

"Know what?" Dad said, still smiling. "You can take our GoPro camera. Bet you can capture a lot of ghosts with it. I can't wait to see what you come back with."

"Go, Sammy!" Mom chanted. "Go, Sammy! I'm so impressed. A whole new you!"

Oh, wow. I didn't expect that.

Go, Sammy, Mom said. *Go right into that haunted house and stay all night. Go find a terrifying ghost. Have fun!*

Mom and Dad had big smiles on their faces, even though they were sending me to my doom. There was no way I could *beg* them to say no. No way I could plead with them to keep me home.

For the next week, I lived in fear. I had terrifying nightmares every night.

But let me tell you the truth . . .

The nightmares weren't *half* as scary as what happened to me Halloween night in that haunted house.

PART TWO

HALLOWEEN NIGHT

Halloween was a shivery, windy night, with a low blanket of rain clouds blocking the moonlight. The sky was an eerie purple, just right for Halloween—or a horror movie. I felt a few cold raindrops on my forehead as Buzzy and I walked to Marple House.

A group of little kids in mummy and Jedi Knight and princess costumes were running down the driveway from the Kochman house on the corner. They were laughing and swinging their trick-or-treat bags as they raced to the next house.

I suddenly had a heavy feeling in my stomach. I knew I was totally jealous of them.

Wouldn't it be better to have *fun* on Halloween instead of risking your life searching out the ghost of a burned-up dead kid inside a cold, damp house?

Buzzy raised his phone to show me a photo of Frizzy, his dog, in some kind of bright-red lobster costume. "We dress him up every year," Buzzy said. "Look. I think he likes it."

The dog looked totally humiliated. He could barely raise his head. But I didn't say that to Buzzy. Why spoil his fun?

"I promised my mom I'd call every hour on the hour," Buzzy said. "She said I had to call so she'd know I'm okay."

"What if our phones don't work in that old house?" I said. "There can't be any Wi-Fi. What if there's no cell service, either?"

Buzzy frowned at me. "You are a serious worrier."

"Tell me something I don't know," I muttered. "Okay. So I'm a worrier. So what?"

"Sammy, did you ever think that maybe spending the night in a haunted house could be *fun*?"

"No," I said. "I never thought it."

We crossed Mulberry. The trees in the lot across the street were swaying from side to side in the gusting wind. A soft rain pattered the sidewalk. I pulled up my hood.

"I've had nightmares every night about this," I said. "Don't laugh at me, Buzzy."

"I wasn't going to laugh," he said.

"I've had really frightening nightmares," I confessed. "The kind where you wake up dripping with sweat and squeezing your pillow."

"About the Marple House?"

I nodded. "Yes. And about the ghost boy."

"Sammy, come on." Buzzy gave me a gentle shove. "Do you really believe he's in there?"

I stopped. The Marple House came into view, rising black against the strange purple sky. "I . . . I don't know what I believe, Buzzy," I stammered.

"Just relax. It's Halloween," Buzzy said, giving me a push forward. "You'll be able to tell your grandchildren you spent Halloween in a real haunted house."

"Huh?" I stared at him. "Grandchildren? I'm twelve years old. I just want to live till I'm thirteen!"

He laughed.

"A couple weeks ago, something happened to me here," I said. I pointed to the house. "I was standing across the street and I . . . I saw something . . . in the house."

Buzzy squinted at me. "What did you see?"

"A face. I mean, I *think* I saw a face. A boy's face. In a window at the top of the house." I pointed. "Way up there."

We walked closer to the house. The swirling wind sent dead, brown leaves dancing around our feet. The trees began to whisper. A bird cawed. It was as if the whole block had suddenly come alive.

"Sammy, think about it," Buzzy said. "A ghost in the daytime sticks his head out the window and watches you?"

"Well, sure. It sounds crazy. But . . . but . . ."

"Yes. Crazy," Buzzy said. "It was one of your dreams. It didn't happen. You dreamed it."

I stopped walking. I grabbed Buzzy's shoulder. "Look."

He followed my gaze to the top of the house. "Do you see it?" I whispered. "A green light? In that window up there?"

Buzzy stopped, and his mouth dropped open.

The front windows of the house were all dark. Except for the top window, where a pulsing green light floated out. And inside the light, I could see a shadow, very still. The shadow of someone peering out from the eerie green.

"Do you see it, too?" I whispered.

Buzzy nodded. "Yes. I see it."

"You see it, too. I'm not making it up. Th-that's the same window," I stammered. "Do you think—?"

"I don't know what to think," Buzzy said.

We stood frozen, staring up at the window. The green light flickered and shifted, but the shadow inside it didn't move.

Suddenly, I had an idea. My dad's GoPro. I pulled it out from my coat pocket. "I . . . I can take a video," I said.

Buzzy lowered his eyes to the camera. "What is that?"

"It's a GoPro Hero. My dad's."

"Awesome. Hurry. Maybe we can make a video

of the ghost before we even go into the house. The others won't believe it."

I couldn't stop the little camera from shaking. I had to grip it in both hands to keep it steady. My heart began to pound in my chest, and a chill froze the back of my neck.

I pointed the lens to the top of the house. My finger fumbled for the RECORD button.

In the tiny window, the pulsing green light appeared to grow brighter. The shadow inside the light still didn't move.

The wind suddenly stopped. A hush fell over the street.

"Are you getting it?" Buzzy asked, his eyes raised to the window. "Are you recording it?"

"I . . . think so," I said. I kept the camera raised in front of me. Held it there for at least another minute. Then I stopped recording and lowered the camera to my side.

"Let's see it," Buzzy said. He grabbed for the camera. "This is so awesome. Let's see what you got."

I swung the camera out of his reach. "Don't grab. Take it easy. You almost made me drop it."

He took a step back. "Sorry. Just excited. Come on. Play the video."

I raised the camera and turned the screen so we both could see it. I reached for the PLAY button.

I let out a cry as something smacked my hand. *"OWWWW!"*

The camera went flying.

Pain stung my hand and shot up my arm.

I heard a sick *craaaack* as the camera smashed into a tree trunk. Buzzy and I watched it slide to the ground.

Buzzy spun me around. "Sammy, why did you do that? Why did you throw your camera?"

"I didn't," I said, trying to shake the pain from my hand. "Something hit me. Something slapped me hard and knocked the camera out."

Buzzy stared hard at me. "I didn't see anything."

We both turned to the tree. "Is the camera okay?"

I dove toward the camera.

My hand still stung from the slap. I dropped to my knees. "It's totally destroyed," I told Buzzy. "Look. It's completely bent." The lens had broken off and lay in the dirt beside the mangled camera body.

Buzzy stepped up beside me, shaking his head. "It had to be the wind," he murmured.

"No way," I said. "Something hit my hand. I mean, like, a real hard slap. It still stings."

"It looked like you threw the camera," Buzzy said. "It hit the tree so hard . . ."

I reached for it. "Whoa." I pulled my hand back. "It's ice-cold, Buzzy. Like it's frozen or something."

He reached down and rubbed his fingers over it. "Weird."

I reached for it again. The camera was too cold to pick up.

I climbed to my feet. "Buzzy, I think I'm going home."

He grabbed my shoulder. "Look." He pointed to the top window of Marple House.

Completely dark now.

A chill ran down my back. A gust of wind sent a pack of dead leaves scuttling along the street like small animals. "I'm definitely going home," I said. "This is too weird."

I started to walk away, but Buzzy raced ahead of me, turned, and blocked my path. "You can't wimp out now. I just realized what the eerie green light in the window up there was about."

"It was a ghost," I said. "A ghost warning us. Letting us know that he's watching us, waiting for us."

Buzzy shook his head. "No. it wasn't a ghost, Sammy. It was Rubin."

My mouth fell open. "Huh?"

"It had to be one of Rubin's jokes," Buzzy said. "He got here early, and he set the whole thing up to scare us. The green light . . . the dark shadow . . . So typical Rubin, right?"

I gazed up at the front of Marple House, now completely dark. My mind was spinning.

"Rubin always has to be first," Buzzy said. "Always has to be better than everyone else. Always has to prove how he's so much smarter than everyone else. It's a typical Rubin joke."

I let out a long breath. "You really think so? He just wanted to get the first scare in?"

"For sure," Buzzy said. "I'll bet you anything he's in that house right now, laughing about what a good scare he gave us."

"Maybe you're right," I said.

"Let's go find out." Buzzy gave me a gentle push, and we began walking toward Marple House. "We'll tell Rubin his little trick in the window didn't scare us at all," Buzzy said.

My heartbeat returned to normal. *Maybe the wind just blew the camera out of my hand,* I thought. We were at the edge of the front lawn when I stopped. I heard a shout behind us.

Buzzy and I spun around—and I saw Rubin halfway down the block, waving to us, followed by Summer and Todd.

"Hey, guys, wait up!" Rubin called. "See any ghosts yet?"

"It . . . it wasn't Rubin," I stammered to Buzzy.

He nodded. "Weird. Really weird."

Our three classmates came hurrying up to us. Rubin carried two long halogen flashlights, one in each hand. Todd had two spotlights on poles over his shoulder. He wore a mask with a big nose, a black mustache, and glasses.

Summer wore a blue down parka, and kept clapping her white fuzzy gloves together. "It's . . . cold," she said.

"It'll be colder in the house," Buzzy said. "Ghosts always make the air colder. It's a scientific fact."

Rubin stepped up to me, lowered his head, and bit me in the neck.

I let out a cry and jumped back.

Rubin grinned. He had a set of rubber fangs in his mouth.

I rubbed my neck. "*Ow.* That hurt."

"Of course it hurt. I'm a vampire."

Summer rolled her eyes. "I told these two guys it's not a costume party. We're here to do serious work."

Todd cupped his hands around his mouth and shouted up to the house. "Hey, ghosts—look out. We're coming to haunt you!"

Rubin shoved him hard, causing him to topple off the curb. Todd struggled to keep hold of his spotlights.

"Hey, shut up, Todd," Rubin snapped. "What do you want to do? Scare the ghosts away?"

"You can't scare ghosts," Todd mumbled. "It's *their* job to scare *you*! Duh."

I thought about the boy who died in the house. The boy who burned so completely no ashes were left. Nothing left at all. And then I thought again about skipping this whole thing and going home.

But Summer was watching me. "I thought maybe you wouldn't come tonight," she said.

"I'm not here. It's my ghost," I said.

She laughed.

Hey! I made her laugh!

Rubin pulled his phone out. "Give me your number, Sammy," he said.

I hesitated. "What for?"

He grinned that awful grin. "So when you get scared and wet yourself, I can call your mommy to come bring you a new pair of jeans."

Todd heehawed at that. Summer just shook her head.

"Rubin, give him a break," Buzzy said.

"Hey, guys." Shamequa came trotting across the street. She carried a large gray suitcase. The words OFFICIAL GHOST HUNTER KIT were stenciled on the side.

Shamequa wore an oversized black wool sweater over black tights. She had a blue wool ski cap pulled low over her forehead. Her breath steamed up in front of her. "Were you waiting for me?"

"Yeah. Sure," Rubin said. "Actually, we were giving Sammy a last chance to chicken out."

Shamequa smiled at me. "Is Rubin on your case already?"

"I can handle him," I lied.

Rubin pulled the wet rubber fangs from his mouth and wiped them on the side of my face. "Thanks, Sammy. I didn't bring a Kleenex."

Summer clapped her furry white gloves together. "Can we go inside? I'm freezing."

We made our way through the opening in the tall hedge and walked up the driveway, our shoes crunching on the gravel. The whole world appeared to grow darker as we stepped into the deep shadow of the house. And the air grew at least ten degrees colder, so cold it burned my face.

Is it this cold because there are ghosts nearby?

I promised myself I wouldn't ask questions like that. But . . . I couldn't help it.

Three broken, cracked steps led up to the front porch. The porch floorboards creaked under our shoes. I helped Shamequa drag the suitcase onto the porch.

Through the front window, I could see only solid black. The front door was tall and wide, painted dark brown, the paint cracked and peeling. Rubin stepped up to the door.

"Anyone home?" Todd shouted. His voice rang out through the frozen air.

Rubin spun around angrily. "Are you going to shut up? Can't you be serious?"

"No, I can't." Todd did a crazy tap dance, his shoes scraping the porch floor. It looked more like stumbling than dancing. I told you, he's a nutcase.

Shamequa laughed. "Todd is right," she said. "It's Halloween night. We should have some fun."

"I thought we wanted to trap some ghosts and get an A for our Science study," Summer said.

"Sure. And have some fun," Shamequa insisted.

Rubin grabbed the large doorknob on the front door. The others huddled close behind him. I hung back at the bottom of the porch stairs.

I watched Rubin turn the knob and lower his shoulder to the door. He groaned as he pushed forward.

The door made a creaking sound.

Rubin jumped back. "Hey!" he uttered a sharp cry.

He lowered his shoulder to the door and gave another push.

I saw the door start to move. But Rubin uttered another cry and leaped back again. He turned to us, his eyes wide with surprise.

"What's wrong?" Buzzy asked.

Rubin swallowed. "Someone is pushing back," he said breathlessly.

I gasped. "Huh? What do you mean?"

Rubin replied in a low voice, almost a whisper. "Someone on the other side of the door is pushing back."

Summer edged away from the group. Shamequa let the suitcase drop to the porch floor. Everyone was suddenly silent, all staring hard at the front door.

I knew what Rubin was doing. It was obvious he was pretending he couldn't open the door just to scare us. Typical Rubin joke. Clever. But not clever enough to fool me.

I gazed at Summer, who was biting her bottom lip, shivering from the cold. This was my chance to impress her.

"Let *me* try the door," I said. I climbed onto the porch and pushed through the others. "Rubin, that's a dumb joke." I shoved him out of my way.

I took a deep breath and grabbed the door-knob. I twisted it and gave the door a hard push. I felt it slide open. Then it slammed back shut.

I jerked my hand off the knob and staggered to the steps. "Oh, wow. Oh, wow," I murmured. "Someone *is* pushing back on the door!"

10

Shamequa shuddered. "This is getting scary, and we're not even in the house yet!" She turned and stepped off the porch, and everyone followed her.

"One thing is sure. The ghost doesn't want us to come in," I said. My voice sounded hollow in the wet night air. I kept my eyes on the door, expecting it to swing open and the ghost to come roaring out. My body was tensed, ready to run.

"Look on the bright side," Summer said. "If there *is* a ghost in there, we'll all get As on our report." Summer is a straight-A student. But I never realized she was so obsessed about grades. Didn't she even stop for a second and think how dangerous this ghost could be?

A rumble of thunder high overhead made me jump. I felt cold raindrops on my forehead.

Todd squinted from Rubin to me. "You two aren't joking? You really felt someone pushing back on the door?"

Rubin motioned to the door. "*You* try it."

Todd shook his head. "No. I believe you."

Maybe we should call the whole thing off. That was my next thought. But I didn't want to be the one to say it.

Another rumble of thunder, this one closer. Raindrops pattered the tall grass of the front lawn. The trees bent and shivered.

"This is why they make so many horror movies about Halloween night," I said.

Rubin grinned at me. "Scared, Sammy? Want someone to hold your hand?"

"Why are we standing here in the rain?" Summer demanded. She pointed. "Let's try that window down there."

I followed her gaze. A window at the corner of the house appeared to be partly open. Summer led the way. Our shoes slid on the rain-wet grass. A jagged bolt of lightning crackled over the roof.

Again I thought of the boy, struck by lightning so long ago. Struck by lightning inside the house and set aflame.

Rubin stepped up to the window and slid his hands under the opening. The whole window appeared to tremble. I guess it was loose in its frame. Rubin grunted as he gave a hard push—and the window slid up with a squeal.

"I'll climb in first," he said. "Then, Shamequa, hoist up the suitcase." He handed me one of his flashlights. "Shine a light into the house as I climb in. If you see a ghost coming for me, scream."

"No problem," I said. I raised the flashlight. It was heavier than I thought it would be. I clicked it on and aimed the white beam of light through the opening in the window.

The light cut through the dark as I waved it around. I could see a large chandelier hanging from the ceiling and some furniture in the center of the room draped in sheets.

Rubin gripped the stone window ledge and lifted himself up to the opening. He grabbed the bottom of the window, then carefully slid his legs into the house. I heard his shoes land with a *thud* on hardwood.

Another jagged bolt of lightning flashed, reflected in the window glass. I gasped. It was as if the whole house suddenly lit up.

"Smells kind of sour in here," Rubin reported, sticking his head out the window. "Like maybe somebody died." He had his eyes on me. He was trying to scare me again. The guy was relentless. He never quit.

Shamequa handed up her suitcase to Rubin, and he helped pull her into the house. Todd slid his spotlights in and climbed in after them. Summer scrambled in next. Buzzy followed.

I grabbed the window ledge and started to pull myself up when I heard Rubin say, "Are we all in?" He slid the window shut.

I pulled my fingers away just in time and dropped back to the ground. "Hey!"

The rain swept down, heavier now. I was getting soaked.

"Hey!" I shouted again. "I don't believe you, Rubin! Open it! Open up, you jerk!"

The window squealed back up. Rubin grinned out at me. "Just messing with you, Sammy."

"Rubin—give him a break!" Buzzy and Summer shouted at once.

"Okay, okay," Rubin muttered. He held out a hand and helped pull me in.

I landed hard, shivering. I tossed my head back, trying to shake the rainwater off. I waved the flashlight around the room. The white light danced over the dark wallpaper, the cracked ceiling, the ghostly chairs and couch covered in dust-smeared sheets.

Tall bookshelves lined the walls. They were empty except for mounds of dust. I figured we were in some kind of den.

Summer hugged herself. "It's colder in here than outside," she said. "I'm frozen right through my coat."

"Our coats are wet," Shamequa said. "We'll be warmer if we take them off."

We obediently pulled off our coats and hats and gloves and piled them on the floor in the corner of the room. Then, without a word, Todd grabbed Rubin's other flashlight, spun away from us, and took off, running toward the doorway.

"Hey!"

"Where are you going?"

"Todd—come back!"

We all shouted after him.

He didn't turn back. I heard his shoes thudding rapidly on the bare floorboards. I could see the beam of light shooting up and down crazily as he ran.

Rubin took off after him. "Todd—what are you doing? Where are you going?"

Gripping the flashlight tightly, I followed them to the next room. Todd stood in the front entryway. He spun to face us. "What's your problem? I went to see if that ghost was still at the front door."

I shone the light up and down over the door. Nothing there.

"Hey, Todd—ghosts are usually invisible," Shamequa said quietly. She stepped up behind Rubin and me.

"I just wanted to see for myself," Todd said.

"Why didn't you tell us first?" Shamequa asked.

Todd shrugged in reply.

"We have to keep together," I said. "For safety."

"But I don't feel safe in the same room with *you*!" Rubin said. His idea of a joke. He head-butted me in the stomach. His other idea of a joke.

I doubled over and staggered back to the wall.

Summer rolled her eyes. "Very mature."

Rubin stuck his tongue out at her.

"Rubin, we're wasting time," I said, rubbing my stomach.

"Sammy is right. Let's go back in the den and make a plan," Shamequa said. "Where are we going to set up our equipment?"

An explosion of thunder shook the house. The flashlight fell from my hand and hit the floor. The light went out. I picked it up and slapped it. I let out a relieved sigh as the light flashed back on.

"Sammy and I think we saw a ghost in the attic window," Buzzy said. "Maybe we should try up there."

"No way," Todd said. "I'm not going up in the attic. That's where lightning strikes first."

"He's right," Shamequa said. "We should stay downstairs. It's safer."

Outside, a wave of rain washed against the front window. Lightning flickered in the distance.

"Maybe a bedroom," Summer said. "Ghosts have to sleep, don't they? Or a room in back. Somewhere a ghost would hide."

Todd pointed. "Let's explore that back hall. See where it leads."

Our shoes scraped the dusty floorboards as we stepped into the narrow hallway. I aimed the beam of light in front of us. It caught a thick nest of cobwebs hanging down over the hallway door.

"Watch out for spiders, Sammy," Rubin warned. I couldn't see his face in the dark, but I knew he was grinning.

Rooms on both sides of the hall had their doors closed. The walls were dark and stained. I moved the light along the molding near the ceiling. More cobwebs stretched out like a fisherman's net.

The webs were covered with dead flies. I stopped to see if I could spot any spiders crawling through the tangles. When I turned, I saw that my friends were far ahead of me.

I started to call to them—but stopped when I felt a rush of cold air at my side. Something soft and cold brushed my face.

And I gasped when I heard a harsh, whispered voice in my ear:

"Sammy, I'm watching you."

11

A chill of fear shook my body. I turned toward the voice.

"Rubin—you're not funny," I growled. "You've *got* to stop picking on me."

No Rubin. No one there.

I raised the light and spun it in a complete circle. "Rubin? Where are you? I know it was you."

I aimed the light into the corners, into the doorways. No one in sight.

The tingle of cold lingered on my face. I could still hear that harsh, raspy whisper in my ear.

"Hey, guys—" I called, my voice shrill and echoing in the long, empty hallway. "Guys?"

My mouth dropped open. A silent cry escaped.

They were gone.

Vanished.

The flashlight trembled in my hand. I raised it and sent the white beam of light to the end of the hall.

Vanished without a trace.

My mind went crazy. *They were swallowed by the house ... Captured by a ghost ... Pulled by whoever haunts this hall into an alternate dimension ... Gone forever ... All of them ...*

I held my breath. And forced the frightening horror-movie ideas from my mind.

"Guys? Where are you?" My voice came out tiny, like a little kid's cry.

Then I heard voices. Someone laughed.

I saw an open door near the end of the hall. A light flickered in the doorway.

My overactive imagination had struck again. They hadn't disappeared. They'd stepped into a room.

My heart was still racing as I hurried to find them. I stepped into the doorway and stopped. I peered into the small, square room. A couch against one wall had a cushion missing and stuffing poking from the back. A low table stood at a tilt because it had only three legs.

My friends were already setting up the ghost-hunting equipment. Shamequa had her suitcase open and was pulling out meters and audio recorders. Todd was standing up his spotlights, one on each side of the room.

Summer turned toward me. "Sammy? Where were you? We thought maybe you decided to leave."

"Huh? Me? Leave?" I said. "Just when the fun is starting?"

Buzzy was helping Shamequa pull out her ghost-hunting tools. "Oops. Just one problem," he said, holding a video monitor between his hands. "Why didn't we think of this? No electricity in this house."

"Not a problem," Shamequa said. "These meters and recorders are all battery-powered. I charged them all before I brought them."

Todd let out a sigh. He shook his head. "Whoa. I'm an idiot. Why didn't I think of it? These spotlights won't work unless I can plug them in."

Rubin laughed. "You're a jerk. You carried them here for nothing." He gave Todd a shove with both hands.

"You're a jerk, too," Todd snapped back. "You didn't think of it, either." He raised his fist and took a step toward Rubin.

Summer rolled her eyes. "Boys, please don't fight."

A flash of lightning filled the window, the light spilling over the room.

"Ghosts probably don't like bright light. I know they like the dark," Shamequa said.

Todd scowled at her. "I guess you know *everything* about ghosts."

"I know you can't plug in lights in an old abandoned haunted house," Shamequa replied.

Why was this going so badly? Why weren't we getting along?

It's true we weren't really friends. Buzzy and

I were friends. But the rest of us . . . well, we were in the same class, but we didn't exactly hang out together.

Miss Flake assigned everyone to this group. Maybe she didn't know that Todd and Rubin hate each other. Maybe she didn't know how much Rubin likes to torture me. Maybe she didn't know that Summer is in the popular girls' group and usually totally ignores the rest of us.

Or maybe Miss Flake *did* know. Maybe she didn't care. Or maybe part of the assignment was for kids who *weren't* friends to get along and do the work.

Or maybe we weren't getting along because we were scared.

"Let's all pitch in and get started," I said. "I know we can do this. I know we can get proof there's a ghost here. This is going to be fun. So come on—let's stop messing around. Let's *do* it, guys."

Rubin laughed. "Listen to Sammy the cheerleader."

"He's just saying we should get our act together," Buzzy said.

Rubin sneered. "Big whoop." He crossed the room and snapped his fingers on my nose.

I tried not to cry out, but it hurt.

Buzzy grabbed Rubin by the shoulders and pulled him back. "Sammy is right. Let's stop

70

fighting and do the work. Do we want to find a ghost or not?"

While this went on, Shamequa and Summer had been quietly working. They had set up the audio and video recorders and the meters and ghost detectors. They lined them up facing the back wall of the room.

Shamequa took the flashlight from me and propped it against one of the meters so it cast its light on the wall. Behind us, the storm raged outside the window. The glass rattled as wind gusts roared and rainwater pounded the house.

"Sit down, everyone," Summer said. "We're ready to start."

Thunder boomed, shaking the house.

Buzzy dropped down on the floor beside me. "Is this the coolest Halloween ever?" he said.

"I guess," I replied.

"Definitely the scariest," Buzzy said.

I started to agree, but Rubin pretended to trip over my legs, and he fell on top of me. "Hey— watch where you're going!" he shouted.

I struggled to squirm out from under him. "You're crushing me!" I cried.

"It was an accident," Rubin insisted. He laughed.

It took us a while to settle down. We sat in a line behind the equipment, our legs crossed, hugging ourselves to try to stay warm.

Shamequa stood, her eyes on the meter and the thermometer. Rubin kept a beam of light from his flashlight steady on the wall.

We sat silently. The only sound now was the howl of the wind outside and the hard patter of rain on the window.

I shifted from side to side. The floor was cold, and the cold seeped up into my legs and my whole body. I gazed at the wall until it became a pale blur in front of my eyes.

Beside me, Buzzy wiped his nose with the sleeve of his sweater. "My nose is numb from the cold," he whispered to me. "Hope the ghost shows himself soon."

"This was all your idea," I whispered back.

Shamequa lowered her head to the digital thermometer. "The temperature is going down," she reported. "It's thirty-two in here."

"That's why we can see our breath," I said.

Summer raised a finger to her lips. We grew silent again.

The windowpane rattled in a sharp blast of wind. Outside, the purple sky had darkened to charcoal black.

I counted silently to one hundred. I thought it might take my mind off how cold it was.

Todd's voice interrupted my count. "Are we having fun yet?" he asked.

"Shut up, Todd," Rubin snapped, swinging

his flashlight and shining the bright light in Todd's eyes.

"Just asking," Todd said. He stretched his arms out, tucked his fingers together, and cracked all his knuckles loudly.

Shamequa rolled her eyes. "Todd, give us a break. This is serious."

"Seriously boring," he muttered. But he settled back down. And we sat there in silence again, staring at the wall and listening to the storm outside.

After ten minutes or so, Summer suddenly spoke up. "Ghosts, hear my voice," she said, breaking the silence. "Ghosts, if you are here, we are friendly."

She paused for a few seconds. Maybe she expected an answer. She stared unblinking at the quivering light beam on the wall. Then, her voice rang out in the empty room again: "Ghosts, if you are here, please give a signal."

One second later, a hard *knock* from behind made us all cry out.

12

Did my heart stop beating?

I think it did.

I know I had to force myself to start breathing again.

No one spoke. We all froze, as if we all had died in place. Time seemed to stop. The sound of that *knock* still rang in my ears.

Silence now. Buzzy grabbed my arm. "Did you . . . hear that?" he stammered.

I nodded. I wasn't sure I could speak yet.

Shamequa stood stiffly, arms crossed tightly in front of her. She had her eyes locked on the meter. The rest of us stayed on the floor, afraid to speak, all listening hard.

And then another *knock* made us gasp and cry out again.

I jumped to my feet. Buzzy stretched out his hand and I helped pull him up.

"It's here," Summer whispered, stepping up

beside Shamequa. She studied the meter. "We all heard it. The ghost replied to me."

Another *knock*.

Rubin swung his light to the door behind us. "It's coming from down the hall, I think. It's coming from the front of the house."

We stood huddled together, staring at one another. Did we really want to go investigate? Finding a ghost seemed like an exciting idea. But when a ghost actually reaches out to you, it's totally terrifying.

"Maybe we should wait for it to come back here," I said. "You know, so we can track it with our equipment."

Rubin ignored me. "We came to prove there's a ghost," he said. "It's signaling to us. It wants us to find it."

He led the way into the hall, swinging a bright beam of light in front of him. Todd, Summer, and Shamequa followed, keeping close together. I walked behind them, chill after chill rolling down my back. I kept my icy hands buried deep in my jeans pockets. My muscles felt all tensed. My whole body was alert.

A hard *knock knock knock* made us stop in the front entryway. The sound rose over the howl of the wind outside.

"It's here," Summer whispered. "I can feel its presence."

I forced myself to keep breathing. My heart was beating so hard, my chest ached.

No one moved. Then, Buzzy pushed past me and Summer and stepped up to the front door. He grabbed the big brass knob, twisted it—and pulled the door open.

And we all uttered cries of shock.

13

Misty Rogers stood there, staring back at us. Her dark hair fell in wet tangles from her hoodie, and raindrops trickled down her forehead. Her down parka was soaked through.

"Sorry I'm late," she said. "Didn't you hear me knocking?"

Buzzy stepped back. Misty burst inside, shaking off rainwater.

We all started to laugh. Not normal laughter. We were all so relieved.

Misty tugged down her hood and struggled to push her hair back. "What's so funny?"

"We thought you were a ghost," Summer told her.

Misty brushed water off her eyebrows. "Have you seen the ghost? Am I too late?"

I shook my head. "You're our first discovery."

Misty blinked in surprise. "Sammy? You're here? We were all betting you wouldn't show."

"Well, you lost your bet," I snapped. That

77

made me angry. Did everyone in the group think I was a coward? I was suddenly glad to be there—just because I proved them wrong.

"We're set up in the back," Shamequa said. "Take off your coat and leave it with ours."

Misty tugged off her backpack, also soaked through. She pulled it open and fumbled inside. "Maybe this will help us," she said. She slid out a long box. Then she let the backpack fall to the floor and she raised the lid on the box.

"Doughnuts!" Rubin cried. "Sweet!" He reached for one.

Misty swung the box out of his reach. "These aren't for us," she said. "These are for the ghost. I was reading this thing online, and it said ghosts totally crave real food."

"Give me one," Rubin insisted. "If we each take only one, there's still a few left for the ghost."

"I'm starving," Todd said, begging with cupped hands. "We forgot to bring any food. If we don't have a doughnut, we'll probably turn into cannibals and eat one another."

"You have a sick mind," Misty said. "Seriously. You need help."

"No, I need a doughnut," Todd insisted.

We all began chanting, "Doughnut! Doughnut! Doughnut!" So Misty passed the box around. And we all gobbled them up in two seconds. Rubin stuffed a whole doughnut into his mouth and swallowed it in one gulp. Todd took tiny mouse bites. He said he wanted to make it last.

There were two doughnuts left in the box. We carried them to the back room and placed the box in front of the video recorder with the lid open.

"If the ghost doesn't want it, I've got dibs on that chocolate one," Rubin said.

"Can we stop talking about the doughnuts?" Shamequa said. She checked the meter and the audio and video recorders. "It's getting late. We have to get back to work."

So we dropped onto the floor again and sat side by side, gazing in silence at the wall. Listening. Waiting. Alert to every sound.

Outside, the rain slowed but the wind continued to howl. Each time the window rattled, I shuddered, expecting it to come crashing down to the floor with glass flying over us.

More silence. The meter didn't click. The temperature didn't move. Shamequa paced back and forth impatiently. Rubin let the light from his flashlight leap around the room. Todd yawned loudly. He cracked his knuckles a few times.

Did we sit like that for an hour? It seemed like *six* hours to me. My legs were stiff and my back ached.

"This is soooo boring," Todd said, breaking the silence.

"Seriously," Buzzy agreed.

I sighed. "I think our study is a flop." I climbed to my feet and shook my left leg, which had fallen asleep. "I think we should give up."

"Me too," Buzzy said. He shivered. "I'm so cold, I think my *bones* are frozen. I feel like a Popsicle. And there's no sign of any ghost. No sign at all."

Summer sighed. "We know the house is haunted. Why doesn't the ghost come out and give us some proof?"

Shamequa sighed, too. "I'll start packing up. This experiment was a total flop."

"What are we going to tell Miss Flake?" Summer asked. "We can't just go in and say we gave up."

"Of *course* we can," Todd insisted. "It's not our fault if the ghost is too shy to show himself."

Summer turned to face us. "Should we vote? How many want to stop now and go home?"

Everyone raised a hand. We all began talking at once. I started to raise my hand—then stopped.

I froze. My heart skipped a beat.

Shamequa had her eyes on me. "Sammy? What's wrong?"

"Hold on," I said. My voice came out in a whisper. "Wait. Just hold on. Didn't you hear it? I think I heard it."

"Heard what?" Rubin demanded.

"I think I heard it," I said. "I think I heard it."

14

Misty grabbed me by the shoulders. "Stop repeating the same thing over and over," she said. "Have you gone crazy?"

"M-maybe," I stuttered. "But I ... I heard something. I definitely heard it."

She tightened her fingers, as if trying to squeeze an answer out of me. "What? What did you hear?"

"A whisper," I managed to say. I slid her hands off my shoulders. "You were all talking. But I heard some words. A whisper. Like hissing in my ears."

Rubin laughed. "Hissing? Maybe it was a snake."

"Not funny," Summer said. Hugging herself, she turned to me. "What were the words? What was the whisperer saying, Sammy?"

I struggled to remember. "Just ... words," I said finally. I was so shocked, I—

"Maybe we captured it on the voice recorder,"

Shamequa said. She moved to the row of equipment. "Maybe we can play it back."

"This could be awesome," Buzzy said. "If we recorded the ghost . . . we could be famous!"

Rubin shook his head. "Why didn't the rest of us hear it? I'll tell you why. Because Sammy imagined it."

"You all started talking," I said. "We were voting on whether to leave, and you all started talking about it. And—"

"Quiet, everyone," Shamequa said. She leaned over the small, square voice recorder. "Let's see what we've got here."

We all huddled close. I jammed my frozen hands into my jeans pockets. I took a deep breath. Had I really heard a ghost?

Shamequa's finger trembled as she pressed PLAY.

Silence.

More silence.

A soft howl in the background. The sound of the wind outside the window.

I held my breath and leaned my head close to the recorder.

More silence. Then crackling static.

And then a terrifying, hoarse whisper: *"You'll never leave this house alive."*

15

I let out a groan. Beside me, Misty murmured, "Oh, wow."

No one moved. Shamequa stopped the recorder. She stood over it, still as a statue.

"Play it again," I said. "Let's hear it again."

Shamequa pushed the button again. Silence, then static.

And then the same terrifying whisper: *"You'll never leave this house alive."*

So clear. So angry.

She played it again.

I gazed from face to face. We had all come here to capture proof of a ghost in the house. But now that we had the proof . . . Now that we'd heard the ghost and its menacing whisper . . . We were too frightened to enjoy our victory.

And then Buzzy let out a cry. He dove past Summer and Todd—and gave Rubin a hard shove with both hands.

Startled, Rubin staggered back and stumbled over the video recorder. "Hey!" he cried out angrily. "What's your problem, Buzzy?" He picked himself up from the floor, both fists tight at his sides.

"You jerk!" Buzzy cried. "I recognize your voice on the recorder. Don't you ever stop with the jokes?"

Rubin's mouth dropped open. "Huh? Are you serious?"

"You recorded that whisper before you came here," Buzzy shouted. "It's not funny, Rubin. You scared us to death and—"

"Shut up!" Rubin cried. He waved both hands in the air. "Time out. Time out, okay? You got it totally wrong, Buzzy. I didn't do that. That was not me."

I turned to Shamequa. "Did Rubin do it? Did he record that whisper on your dad's recorder?"

She shook her head. "I don't see how he could."

"No way!" Rubin protested. "You saw Shamequa unpack that recorder. No way I ever touched it."

Buzzy retreated, his stare still accusing Rubin.

Todd moved to the audio recorder. He gazed at Shamequa. "So . . . if Rubin didn't whisper those words, that means . . . That means we have our proof."

"Yes!" Summer cried happily. She slapped

Todd a high five. "We've captured the ghost. We've proven that this house is haunted. We really are ghost hunters!"

She and Todd cheered. Todd reached for Summer's hands, and they did a short victory dance together. Misty joined in.

I wasn't quite ready to celebrate. For one thing, the ghost said we'd never leave the house alive. Maybe the others were forgetting that part, but I wasn't.

"Miss Flake is going to freak out," Shamequa said. She started to pack the video recorder back into the suitcase.

"No. wait," I said.

"Can you make copies of the ghost whisper?" Summer asked. "I think we should each have a copy."

"No problem," Shamequa replied. She picked up the audio recorder.

"Wait. Come on. Wait," I insisted. "Can we listen to it one more time?"

Summer shivered. "Why? We've heard it, Sammy. Don't you want to get home? We're all freezing to death."

I motioned to Shamequa. "Just play it one more time. I . . . I still think it's Rubin. Just one more time."

She shrugged and pushed the PLAY button.

We all stood staring at the recorder. Silence at first, then the crackling static. Then more static.

The crackling grew louder, then faded. The recording ended.

"Hey!" Summer was the first to speak. "Back it up. What happened to the ghost voice?"

Shamequa pushed the button again. The static played, rising and falling like the wind.

No voice. No whisper.

"I . . . I don't understand it," Shamequa stammered. "I'm playing the same part of the recording. But . . ."

"But the voice is gone." Summer finished her sentence.

"But . . . we all heard it," Misty said. "We know it was real."

"Gone," Summer muttered, shaking her head.

And then the ghost detection meter began to click. From the open suitcase. It clicked slowly at first, like the second hand on a clock. Then it picked up speed, clicking a rapid drumbeat.

A shadow danced on the wall. And then an animal howl tore through the room, like a furious wolf.

Summer and Misty screamed. Todd ducked as a shadow leaped off the wall and appeared to rocket toward him. He hit the floor and scrambled out of the way.

Rubin backed to the wall. His dark eyes wide with terror.

The meter clicked and the shadow danced and the shrill howl rang out again.

Not the wind. Not the howl of the wind. But a terrifying cry *inside the room*.

"Let's get *out* of here!" I screamed. "Everyone—move!"

But something held me in place. I spun toward the door but I couldn't move.

And that's when I started to feel seriously weird.

16

It started with an icy tingle at the back of my neck. A prickling on my skin that felt different from the shivery feeling I'd had all night. And it buzzed. I mean, I could hear a soft buzz—like an electrical charge—as the chill spread over the back of my neck.

And then the cold swept down my body, like an avalanche of snow. That's what it felt like. Deep snow covering me, slipping down my chest, my arms, my legs.

I was too frightened to cry out at first. Locked in total panic. But then I tried to call to the others—and no sound came from my throat.

As I struggled to signal to them, I could feel the buzzing current shooting through me. My head throbbed. Began to feel heavy. I could feel it freezing. My whole head. Frozen and hard like a block of ice.

I tried to wave my arms. To get their attention. To scream. To kick. To do *something*.

I was buried in the cold. The icy heaviness pressed down on me. The electrical buzz rang in my ears.

I couldn't move. I couldn't breathe.

I'm a snowman. I'm as heavy and cold—and dead—as a snowman.

Where were the others? Why weren't my friends helping me? Were they frozen, too?

Gripped in horror, I tried to scream again. But my face was frozen hard. I couldn't even open my mouth.

17

And then suddenly, the weight of the cold slowly lifted. I could feel myself getting lighter. Feel my head clearing.

My vision was suddenly sharp. The room came back into focus. I blinked. I shook my head.

I tossed my whole body around, struggling to shake off the remaining cold.

Still stunned, I swung my arms and examined my hands. I bent my knees.

I could feel the warmth slowly rise from my feet, up my legs, over my waist, my chest.

I'm thawing. The cold is melting, fading away.

I blinked a few more times and rubbed the back of my neck. Still cold and stiff.

Trembling, I glanced up and realized everyone was staring at me.

"Sammy—are you all right?" Buzzy asked, hurrying over to me. "You scared us. You looked so weird."

I cleared my throat. "I . . . felt weird," I said. "All of a sudden, I—"

"Know why you looked weird?" Rubin interrupted. "Because you're weird."

"Rubin, get off his case," Buzzy said. He turned to me. "Do you feel sick?"

"I felt cold," I said. "Cold all over. I couldn't move or anything. Like I was packed in ice. It . . . it happened so quickly. The cold just washed over me and . . . and buried me."

I expected them to make fun of me. I figured they'd say, *Same old wimpy Sammy.*

But they watched me with serious expressions. No one said a word, not even Rubin.

"Let's get out of here," Todd said finally. "It's almost midnight, and this house is getting creepier and creepier."

Summer sighed. "We don't have our proof. We don't have anything to show Miss Flake."

"I don't care," Todd said. He gathered up his spotlights. "I'm out of here. If there are ghosts in this house, I wish them a happy Halloween."

Misty and Summer helped Shamequa pack her equipment back in the suitcase. Rubin kept a light on them as they worked. Every few seconds, he swung the flashlight around and shined the light into my eyes, just to be annoying. He laughed every time.

No one talked. What was there to say? Our

ghost hunt was a failure. Yes, we heard a whispered voice. Yes, we saw a shadow and heard weird howls. But we had no proof. No proof at all.

I was as disappointed as everyone else. But I was also happy to be getting out of that creepy house safe and sound. And pleased that I had proven to the others that I was as brave as they were.

Sure, Rubin would continue to pick on me and make my life hard. But I had proven something to myself.

We gathered up our coats, which were still damp from the rain. Then we hurried out the front door. Rubin slammed it hard behind us.

The rain had stopped, and a pale half-moon hung between the clouds. The air smelled cool and fresh. Puddles glistened on the driveway as we made our way to the street.

We said very quick good-byes. I think we were all eager to go home and get warm. Buzzy and I crossed the street and headed toward our block.

"You feeling okay?" Buzzy asked. "You were looking pretty strange in there."

"Yeah. Fine," I said. "I think I just caught a chill or something. It was so cold in there."

"Shame we didn't get our proof," Buzzy murmured.

"Yeah. Shame," I said.

As my house came into view on the next block, I was happy to put an end to this Halloween night and our stay in the old haunted house.

I didn't realize that my life was about to change forever.

PART THREE

A FEW DAYS LATER

18

"Let's begin our discussion, everyone," Miss Flake shouted over the voices and laughter in the room. Lunch period had just ended. A seventh grader had passed around a big basket of leftover Halloween candy. And we were all pretty hyper from the chocolate.

"I hope you all read the unit in your texts about the early exploration of the West." Miss Flake motioned with both hands for us to quiet down.

She dropped onto the edge of her desk and tapped her foot impatiently, waiting for all the talking to stop. She picked at something on the sleeve of her white sweater. Then she called for quiet again.

I sat in the middle of the back row. I felt pretty safe back there. I hate class discussions, and I hate being called on. The main reason is Rubin Rubino.

Every time I say something in class, he makes a joke about it. He thinks it's a riot to imitate me and put me down and make fun of everything I say. Miss Flake has warned him about it, but Rubin doesn't quit. And lots of times, he gets big laughs at my expense.

I finally decided the best way to stop Rubin's jokes was for me to stop saying anything in class. So, the middle of the back row is the best place for me to sit. I can just duck my head low behind Derek Delaney, a big mountain of a kid who sits right in front of me, and Miss Flake never sees me to call on me.

"Sammy, did you read the chapter?" Buzzy whispered from the seat next to me.

I nodded. "Yeah. Sure. Did you?"

"I left my textbook in my locker yesterday," Buzzy said in a loud whisper. "So I couldn't read it."

"Maybe she won't call on you," I whispered back.

"So who can tell me why the early pioneers were so eager to explore the American West?" Miss Flake asked. Her eyes surveyed the room. "What were their reasons? They had a lot of reasons for leaving their homes in the East and heading west, right? What were they?"

Several kids raised their hands. Rubin didn't raise his. He just shouted out, "They wanted to visit Hollywood!"

That got a big laugh. Miss Flake laughed, too.

She thinks Rubin's jokes are funny, and she lets him shout out stuff all the time.

Very annoying.

Summer, sitting in the first row, right in front of the teacher, raised her hand. "Economic opportunity," she said.

Miss Flake leaned toward her. "What does that mean?"

"They wanted to find work?" Summer answered. "Like start a ranch or farm or something."

"Yes, that's good," Miss Flake said. "Many people thought they could settle on big plots of land and get rich from farming or ranching."

Buzzy waved his hand in the air. "And don't forget the gold."

Miss Flake nodded. "Yes. The Gold Rush. Everyone desperate to get to California, right? And dig up a fortune of gold. Of course, that happened later. Who can tell me when the Gold Rush began?"

Several kids raised their hands. I lowered my head behind Derek Delaney and tried to hunch myself as skinny as I could.

Peeking out from behind Derek, I could see Miss Flake staring in my direction. Was I imagining it? No. She was watching me for some reason.

I ducked down even lower and almost fell out of my chair.

Misty Rogers was talking about the Gold Rush and how the railroad was important for bringing people to the West. Miss Flake asked more questions about covered wagon trains.

I peeked out from behind Mountain Delaney. The teacher was definitely staring at me. What was up with that? Was she waiting for me to join the discussion?

I could feel my cheeks turning red. I turned away from her. I saw Rubin on the aisle in the second row, grinning at me. He puckered his lips and spit a big wad of chewing gum at me. It landed on the front of my shirt and stuck there.

Did Miss Flake see him do that? No.

"I'd like you to read the next chapter in class right now," she said. "Some quiet reading. And you'd better take notes, because this chapter is going to be on the quiz on Friday."

Chairs scraped as kids reached for their backpacks to get their History texts. I tugged the gum off my shirt. It left a big wet spot. I stuck the gum under the desk and started to open my book to the chapter.

"Sammy?" Miss Flake called. "Could I see you for a moment?"

Uh-oh. I was about to find out why she was staring at me.

19

She sat at her desk, tapping a pencil eraser against a pile of books. I could see that her eyes were on the wet spot on the front of my shirt.

I stepped around to the side of the desk. "Did you want me?"

She scooted her chair closer. "Sammy, do you feel uncomfortable in my class?" she asked in a whisper.

"Excuse me?" I blinked. I wasn't expecting that question. "Well . . ."

She tapped the pencil eraser a little harder on the desktop. Her eyes locked on mine, as if she was trying to read my mind. "We have class discussion time every day," she said, still whispering.

Summer kept looking up from her textbook. I knew she could hear what Miss Flake was saying. I could feel my cheeks turning red.

"Part of your grade is class participation,"

Miss Flake said. "And you never participate. You never join in, Sammy. Is there a problem?"

Yes. A definite problem. His name is Rubin Rubino. I can't join in because every time I do, he makes me look like a jerk.

That's what I wanted to say. But *no way* I'd admit that I was terrified of Rubin.

"I . . . I'm just kind of shy, I guess," I stammered. "I don't like to speak in class."

She studied me for a long moment. "You have to work on that, Sammy. Okay?"

I nodded.

"You need to join in," she said. "I know you do your homework. And I know you know the answers to most of the questions. So . . . try to raise your hand more, okay?"

"Okay," I said quickly. What else could I say?

As I walked back to my seat, Rubin stuck his foot into the aisle and tripped me.

I stumbled forward, grabbed at air, trying to keep myself up—and landed with a loud "*Ooooof*" on my stomach.

The class went wild, laughing and hooting and heehawing. As I slowly raised myself up, I saw Summer turn in her seat, her head tossed back in laughter. And I wanted to collapse back onto the floor. Maybe curl up into a little ball and roll away.

"Rubin! That was terrible!" Miss Flake was on her feet, her face twisted in anger.

Rubin, grinning of course, shrugged. "It was an accident, Miss Flake. A total accident."

More wild laughter.

I slumped back to my seat. My heart was pounding angrily in my chest. I gritted my teeth.

I pictured myself racing down the aisle, grabbing Rubin by the front of his shirt, jerking him from his chair, and pounding him . . . pounding him until he stopped grinning.

But, of course, I could never do anything like that. I'm a good guy. That's my whole thing. I'm always good. I always do the right thing.

But my anger made my whole brain throb. I started to sit down. I was so crazed, I totally missed the chair. "Hey!" I cried out as I fell again. Landed hard on my butt. So hard, I bounced twice. The chair fell over backward with a loud clatter.

Now everyone went berserk. Laughing and shouting.

Miss Flake took a few steps toward me, her face tight with worry. "Are you okay?"

I grunted. I was still on the floor.

"We should get him a floor mat like in the kindergarten," Rubin shouted. "He doesn't know how to work a chair."

It wasn't that funny, but everyone went wild anyway.

Miss Flake gazed around, looking confused. She knew she had totally lost control of the class. The roar of voices and laughter rang off the walls.

"Quiet, people!" Miss Flake shouted. "Falling off a chair is very funny. But we need to settle down now."

It took a while, but everyone finally stopped talking and laughing.

"Let's get it together, everyone," Miss Flake said. "We all like to yuk it up when someone has a funny accident. But let's get on with class."

I eased myself carefully into my chair. I gazed around the room. At least no one was watching me now.

"That's better, guys," Miss Flake said. She opened the History textbook. "Why don't we discuss the chapter you read last night? Summer, do you want to start by telling us what the chapter was about?"

Summer started to talk. I tried to listen, but something strange was happening to me.

I suddenly heard a whispered voice, a boy's voice right by my ear. He said, *"Climb onto your desk and do jumping jacks."*

I looked around. "Buzzy—what did you say?"

Buzzy turned in surprise. He had been listening intently to Summer. He squinted at me. "I didn't say anything," he whispered.

I turned back to the front of the room. And I heard the whispered instruction again: *"Climb onto your desk and do jumping jacks."*

104

I blinked a few times. I glanced around. Where was the voice coming from?

Suddenly, I realized I had sprung to my feet. As Summer continued to describe the History chapter, I climbed onto my desk. I stood on the desktop and raised both arms high.

"Sammy?" Miss Flake shouted. "What on earth are you doing?"

20

Miss Flake's voice seemed very far away. I saw the kids all turn to see what she was shouting about. I heard gasps of surprise and a few sharp cries. But the kids' faces were suddenly a blur, and their voices were muffled and faint.

"Sammy? Get down! We're having a class discussion. What are you *doing*?"

I bent my knees and jumped into the air. My shoes landed heavily on the desktop. I heard more gasps and cries of surprise. I began to jump in rhythm, waving my arms up over my head, then down at my sides.

Jump. Arms up, arms down. Jump. Arms up, arms down.

As I jumped, my brain spun. Why was I doing this? Had I totally lost it? Why couldn't I stop?

"Sammy? Sammy?"

Was Miss Flake shouting my name over and over?

I saw her running down the aisle toward my desk. And I heard wild laughter all around and startled voices.

Jump. Arms up, arms down.

My heart pounded in my chest. My whole body tingled. I shut my eyes and concentrated. I had to end this. I had to stop . . .

My shoes landed with a thud. I brought my arms to my sides. I finally stopped jumping.

Miss Flake tugged at my jeans leg. "What are you doing? Why did you disrupt the class? Get down. Sammy—get down right now."

The teacher tugged my jeans leg again. "Come down. This instant!" she insisted.

And then I heard the whispered voice again: *"Pretend you're playing 'Jingle Bells' on the flute."*

21

I gazed around. Where was the voice coming from?

Of course, I instantly thought of Rubin. But he was halfway across the room.

"Pretend you're playing 'Jingle Bells' on the flute."

It sounded as if the voice was inside my head. It was definitely a boy's voice, a voice I didn't recognize.

I raised both hands and curled my fingers to make a pretend flute. And I began to toot "Jingle Bells" as loud as I could.

"Toottoottoot, toottoottoot, toot toot TOOT toot toot."

I could see kids toss back their heads and laugh. A few were laughing so hard, their faces turned bright red. Some kids slapped their desktops and stomped the floor in rhythm with my tooting.

Miss Flake had her hands pressed to the sides

of her face. Her eyes were wide. Her mouth hung open. "Sammy—stop it! Sammy—you know I enjoy a good joke. But this is CRAZY!"

"Toottoottoot, toottoottoot, toot toot TOOT toot toot."

I bobbed my head as I tooted, moving my pretend flute up and down.

Suddenly, Miss Flake spun toward me. She reached up and wrapped her arms around my legs. She pulled hard, as if she were tackling me in a football game.

"Toottoot toottoot . . ." I didn't quit as I started to go down.

She gripped me tightly and pulled me off the desktop. We both stumbled backward. She smacked the wall and her hands slid off me.

I struggled to catch my breath. I squinted until her angry, confused face came into focus. Kids were screaming with laughter. Some of them were copying me, tooting their own flutes as loud as they could.

The teacher stepped away from the wall. Breathing hard, she grabbed my wrists. "Follow me. Into the hall."

My brain was spinning in my head. I felt totally dazed.

She pulled me outside the noisy classroom into the hall. The air was cooler out here. The hall was empty, except for a girl way down at the other end, shoving books into her locker.

Miss Flake backed me into the wall. She was still breathing hard. Her ponytail had come loose and a thick strand of hair had fallen over her forehead.

Her eyes studied me for a long moment. "You know, Sammy," she started, "I asked you to participate more in class. But not like that!"

I opened my mouth but no sound came out.

"Are you feeling okay?" She wrapped a hand over my forehead—and pulled it away quickly. "Hey—you're ice-cold. Your forehead is ice-cold."

I felt my forehead. She was right. It felt like it had been in a freezer.

Weird.

"Sammy, can you explain what just happened back in my classroom?" She spoke softly, her eyes studying me with concern.

"Not really," I said.

What else could I say? *No way* I could explain it.

She nodded. "Okay. Okay." I could see she was thinking hard. "I'm going to send you to the nurse's office, Sammy. I think Mrs. Bradley should see you. Your head doesn't feel right. And you're acting so strangely, I think you might be sick."

She waited for me to reply. But I didn't know what to say. Finally, I said, "Maybe."

She glanced back toward the classroom. Through the open door, I could hear kids still laughing and shouting and tooting pretend flutes. "I'd better get back in there," Miss Flake said. "Do you want me to walk you to Mrs. Bradley's office?"

I shook my head. "No. I can walk there. Thanks." The nurse's office was downstairs, a few doors past the lunchroom. I turned toward the stairs.

"Come back and report after you see her," Miss Flake said.

I nodded. "No problem."

But what could Mrs. Bradley say?

22

The scrape of my shoes on the hard floor rang in my ears as I made my way down the empty hall. I still didn't feel right. My head felt heavy. I was off-balance. I couldn't walk a straight line. I kept zigzagging even though I didn't feel dizzy.

A million thoughts swept through my mind. I tried to figure out why I did those crazy things. I'm too shy and too afraid of Rubin to even *speak* in class. So why did I jump up on my desk, do jumping jacks, then toot like a crazy person on a pretend flute?

Only a crazy person would do that. But I'm not crazy. I'm the most normal, least troubled, best-behaved kid in school. Ask anyone.

So suddenly I hear a voice telling me to do insane things—and I don't refuse. I do it.

Why? It was a total mystery to me. I couldn't think of an answer. No answer at all.

Mrs. Bradley's office door was half-closed. The

door had a white glass window with the word NURSE stenciled in black. I knocked softly on the window.

"Come in," she called immediately.

I swung the door open and stepped into the room. She was hunched behind her desk, eating a sandwich over a paper plate.

"I can come back later," I said. "If you're eating . . ."

"No. Sammy. Come in." She motioned me with her free hand.

Mrs. Bradley is pretty old. She has frizzy white hair that looks a lot like a Brillo pad bouncing on her round head, dark round eyes that always seem to be squinting at you behind black-framed eyeglasses, pink cheeks, and a nice smile.

She doesn't wear a nurse's uniform. Today she was wearing a long plaid skirt and a white top buttoned to the collar.

The office is narrow. Just enough room for a cot for a kid who needs to lie down or take a nap. Her small desk. And a tall cabinet where she keeps her medicines and supplies. She has a framed diploma on her wall from her school. It's next to a photo of Gunther, her golden Lab.

She set down her sandwich half and wiped tuna fish off the side of her mouth. "Sammy? What can I do for you?"

"Miss Flake sent me here," I said.

She wrinkled her forehead. "You're not feeling well?"

"Well . . . I'm feeling a little weird," I said.

And then a voice whispered in my ear: *"Take her sandwich and stuff it into her mouth."*

23

No way, I told myself.

I'm not going to do it. I can't do that.

I can fight this.

I shoved my hands deep into my jeans pockets. I held my breath.

I was sure I could defeat the boy's voice in my head. I knew he couldn't force me to do something like that.

"Sammy? Are you okay?" Mrs. Bradley's eyes squinted at me through her thick eyeglasses.

"Well . . ."

The voice whispered again inside my head: *"Take her sandwich and stuff it in her mouth."*

I stepped up to Mrs. Bradley's desk. I grabbed half of her tuna fish sandwich and I stuffed it into her open, startled mouth.

Her head snapped back, her eyes went wide, and she started to choke and gag. She jerked the sandwich from her mouth. Still sputtering, she tossed it onto her desk.

Mrs. Bradley leaped to her feet and angrily slammed her fist on the desktop. The sandwich went flying to the floor.

I stood there openmouthed, shaking my head. I couldn't believe what I had just done. My head felt suddenly light, and my legs started to tremble.

"Sammy!" The nurse screamed my name. "Sammy, have you gone *crazy*? Did you think that was *funny*?"

"N-no," I stammered.

"Then why did you do that? Tell me—why?" She brushed a chunk of tuna fish off her cheek.

"I . . . don't know," I said. My brain whirred. *Should I tell her about the voice?*

"Come here. Let me see if you have a temperature," Nurse Bradley said. "That wasn't like you at all. You have always been the best-behaved sixth grader in school."

She pressed a hand over my forehead. "Your head is cold," she said. "You're not running a temperature." She motioned me to the cot. "Sit down, Sammy. Tell me what just happened here."

I sat on the edge of the cot. I didn't know what to do with my hands. I clasped them in front of me. Then I lowered them to the cot and leaned back on them.

"I'm waiting." Mrs. Bradley said softly. "Tell me what's troubling you, Sammy." She kept her eyes on me as she brushed sandwich crumbs off her desktop.

"Well . . . I heard a voice," I started.

She blinked. "A voice?"

"Yes. Inside my head." I took a deep breath. "The voice told me to shove the sandwich into your mouth. I didn't want to. Really. But I couldn't resist what the voice told me to do."

She stared hard at me. She didn't move.

"I tried to fight it," I said. "But . . . I couldn't."

She kept her hard stare on me for a long time. Then she put both hands on the edge of her desktop. "That's quite a story," she said finally.

I swallowed. "Well . . ."

"Since when do you make up stories, Sammy?" she said. "I'm just stunned. I'm so surprised that you would tell me something as crazy as that."

She sat down behind her desk and lowered her voice. "Do you want to tell me the truth now? Do you want to tell me the *real* reason you did that to me?"

I swallowed again. My mouth was suddenly as dry as sand. "Mrs. Bradley, really—" I started.

"Was it some kind of dare?" she demanded. "Tell the truth, Sammy. Did another kid dare you to do it?"

I shook my head. "No. Not a dare," I murmured.

I realized I was dumb for trying to tell her the truth. Why would anyone believe that a boy's voice had taken control of my brain and was forcing me to do ridiculous things?

"It's Rubin Rubino, isn't it?" Mrs. Bradley said, studying me. "Rubin dared you to do it, and you're too afraid of him to say no."

I probably should blame it on Rubin, I thought. *It would get him into major trouble, and that would be fun.*

But I couldn't do that, even to my archenemy.

"No. Not Rubin," I murmured, lowering my gaze to the floor. "Rubin didn't dare me to do anything."

Mrs. Bradley scratched her springy white hair. I could see she was thinking hard. "Why don't you lie down on the cot for a short while, Sammy?" she said. "Take your shoes off. Relax for a few minutes. I want to talk to Miss Flake about you. While I'm gone, try to clear your head."

I saw that I had no choice. I leaned down to untie my sneakers. And I heard the voice whisper: *"Pick up the pillow from the cot, tear it open, and eat the stuffing."*

24

I dove for the pillow and slid the pillowcase off. Then I dug my fingers into the soft cloth covering and ripped it apart.

"Sammy?" Behind me, Mrs. Bradley jumped to her feet again. Her chair slid hard into the office wall.

I tore a chunk of foam rubber stuffing off the pillow and jammed it into my mouth.

Yuck. It tasted terrible. Bitter and disgusting. I chewed fast. It was so dry, chunks stuck to my tongue and the roof of my mouth. Somehow, I choked it down and stuffed another big hunk into my mouth.

"Stop it! Stop it!" the nurse shrieked.

She grabbed my shoulders and pulled me to my feet. Then she spun me around and made a wild grab for the foam rubber.

I twisted it out of her reach.

"Sammy—please! Stop it! Put it down! Stop it!"

I chewed frantically. I was panting hard. The awful, bitter taste was making me gag.

With a hard tug, Mrs. Bradley pulled the big hunk of pillow stuffing from my hands. She tossed it out into the hall.

I choked down the last bite of foam rubber.

We were both gasping for breath now. My heart was pounding in my chest. Her face was as red as a tomato. I kept spitting, frantic to get the taste of the foam rubber from my mouth.

Neither one of us spoke for a long time. We were both recovering. Both unable to speak.

Finally, she pulled her chair back to the desk, sat down, and quickly scribbled some notes onto a pad. "Sammy, are you sure Rubin didn't put you up to doing this?" she said finally.

I shook my head. "I swear. He didn't."

She pulled a narrow white thermometer from her desk drawer. "Put this under your tongue. I want to have your correct temperature for the record."

I slid it under my tongue.

She wrote some more on her pad. "This is very strange behavior," she said, eyes on her writing. "Very strange. Not like you at all." She sighed. "I don't think I can deal with this on my own."

The thermometer made a *ding ding* sound. She slid it from my mouth and brought it close to her face to read it. She squinted at it for a long time before lowering it to her side.

"This is impossible," she said, her voice just above a whisper. "It reads 60.5."

My mouth dropped open. "Huh? 60.5?"

She nodded. "That can't be. You wouldn't be alive with that temperature. My thermometer must be broken."

She shoved the thermometer back in the desk drawer. Then she motioned again to the cot. "Lie down, Sammy. Go ahead. Lie down. And don't try to eat anything, okay?"

I obediently stretched out on my back on the cot. The room was spinning around me. I didn't feel like myself at all. I had a heavy feeling of dread in my stomach. I wasn't used to being in trouble—and I knew I was in *major* trouble now.

Mrs. Bradley gripped her pen above her writing pad. "Tell me your parents' phone numbers. I'm going to call them and tell them to come get you."

I groaned. "Do you have to call them?"

She nodded. "You're worrying me, Sammy. Your parents need to know what's going on with you."

"Well . . ." Mom and Dad weren't going to like getting a call from school. It had never happened before. They would definitely be surprised—and upset.

"Come on, Sammy. Give me the numbers," she insisted.

But before I could answer, her desk phone rang.

She picked up the receiver and started to talk. I slowly pulled myself up on the cot. She turned away from me, the phone pressed to her ear.

I didn't hesitate. I leaped up and as silently as I could, tiptoed from her office. I held my breath until I made it into the hall. I listened for her to call to me. But she was still on the phone. She didn't see me escape.

I started to trot down the long hall. I didn't know where I was going. I guess I planned to go home. I was still not thinking clearly.

I was nearly to the back exit when the bell rang to end the school day. Kids came pouring out of their classrooms. The hall filled with shouts and laughs and the squeal of lockers opening.

My jacket! I was in such a hurry to escape, I'd forgotten to get it. Through the back windows, I glanced at the sky. Cloudy and dark. Maybe snow on the way.

I turned and hurried back down the hall. I was desperate to get to my locker without Mrs. Bradley seeing me. Kids began to stampede toward the exits. Someone bumped me hard from behind. Rubin. He laughed and trotted ahead of me.

I ducked behind a group of girls when Miss Flake came walking by. I didn't want her to see me, either. I heard Todd calling to me, but I kept walking.

I pulled open my locker door and tugged out

my parka. I glanced both ways. No sign of Mrs. Bradley. I slammed the locker shut and pulled the coat over my head so I couldn't be seen.

Someone tapped me on the shoulder.

Startled, I spun around. "Summer?"

Summer Magee smiled at me. Those sky-blue eyes twinkled above her dimpled cheeks. "Sammy, you were so funny in class today," she said.

"Uh . . . thanks." I couldn't believe it. Summer Magee just said something nice to me? She actually came over to talk to me?

Her smile grew even warmer. "You were a riot, Sammy. Everyone thinks you were a riot. I never knew you were so funny."

"Thanks," I said again.

"See you tomorrow." She tossed her blond hair behind her head, flashed me one more smile, then took off.

I stood there stunned for a few seconds. Those were the nicest words Summer had ever said to me.

I might have stood there longer. But I heard teachers' voices around the corner. I spun the dial on my locker lock, ducked my head under the parka hood, and ran off.

Mom was waiting for me at the front door. She had her worried face on. "Sammy, are you sick? The nurse called me from school. She said you might need a doctor."

"No, I'm not sick," I said. I slipped past her, into the front hall. I started to hang my parka in the front closet.

"Mrs. Bradley called me. She thinks you are sick," Mom said. She had her arms crossed tightly in front of her sweater. Her eyes were examining me, looking for signs of illness.

"I did some funny things in class today," I said.

"Funny things?"

Should I tell her the truth? Should I tell her what happened?

Yes, I decided. I took a deep breath. "Mom, this voice in my head . . . It told me to stand on my desk and do jumping jacks. Right in the middle of class. Then it told me to take the nurse's tuna fish sandwich and stuff it in her mouth."

Mom gasped. "Oh, no. Oh, please, no. And did you do those things?"

I nodded. "I couldn't resist. I had to."

She made a choking sound. "I'm . . . I'm so sorry, Sammy. It's not your fault."

"Huh? Not my fault? Mom, what do you mean?"

"Your father and I never should have let you go to that haunted house on Halloween. We knew it was the kind of thing that terrifies you. But we thought . . . I guess we thought it might make you braver."

I just stared at her. I didn't know what to say.

"Sammy, I think being there that night upset you. I think it was too much for you. Some people just don't like scary things, and you're one of them. Your father and I have to realize that. We . . . pushed you too hard. And it's made you have these episodes."

"Episodes?"

She felt my forehead. "Perfectly normal. You'll be okay. We'll discuss this more when your father gets home. Go take a nap for an hour or so. You're going to be fine."

I nodded and made my way down the back hall to my room. I was totally surprised that Mom blamed that night in Marple House for my problem. Could she be right?

I sat down on the edge of my bed and punched Buzzy's number on my phone. It went right to voice mail.

I tossed my phone down. I didn't feel like taking a nap. I was too tense, too wired, too confused. I sat there hunched on the edge of the bed for a long time. Thinking. Waiting.

Waiting to hear the voice again.

"Come on, voice," I murmured out loud. "Come on. Are you there? Speak up. Come on. Let me hear you. I'm listening. Are you there?"

25

The next morning, Buzzy stopped me at the front door to the school. "Did you hear? Our field trip was canceled," he said.

"Canceled? You mean no maple syrup? No pancakes?"

He shook his head. "We're having an assembly instead. The mayor is coming to talk."

I rolled my eyes. "Bor-ing."

"Tell me about it," Buzzy muttered.

I heard other kids grumbling about the canceled field trip as I walked through the crowded front hall to my locker. I shoved my backpack into the bottom of the locker and pushed the door closed.

When I turned, I saw Summer Magee smiling at me again. She wore a long-sleeved blue top that matched her eyes perfectly. Her dangly plastic earrings jangled as she tilted her head at me.

"Sammy, are you going to do more funny stuff today?" she asked.

126

I sure hope not. That's what I thought.

But I said, "Maybe. Maybe I will. We'll see."

That answer seemed to please her. She flashed me another smile, then turned and hurried away.

Summer had ignored me for three years. And now she seemed ready to form a Sammy Baker Fan Club. And all because of my weirdo behavior.

As I made my way to the morning assembly, I just kept asking myself: *What if it happens again? What if I keep doing terrible, crazy things? Will I be kicked out of school? What will happen to me?*

So many questions, my head was spinning as I stepped into the auditorium. I took a seat in the third row. Also in my row were Buzzy and Summer and Rubin.

Our principal, Mr. Harkness, introduced Mayor Springfield. The mayor pulled out a speech from his suit pocket and leaned over the podium onstage, droning on about how city government works, in a soft voice I could barely hear.

Kids were whispering and shifting in their chairs and laughing over private jokes. Mr. Harkness had to interrupt the mayor twice and warn us all to be a good audience.

I could feel my eyelids growing heavy. I think maybe I started to doze off. But I didn't really fall asleep—because the voice suddenly returned.

I jerked up straight as I heard a whispered command:

"Go up onstage and help the mayor. Do a crazy tap dance, Sammy."

Buzzy grabbed my arm. "Hey, are you okay?"

I nodded. I was too startled to answer Buzzy.

"Go onstage and do a tap dance," the voice repeated. The boy's voice. *"Swing your arms and crow like a rooster."*

I climbed to my feet.

"Hey, Sammy—sit down!" Buzzy called.

I ignored him and pushed my way along the seats, stepping over sneakers, forcing kids to move. I stumbled into the aisle, caught my balance, and began to trot to the stage.

"Help the mayor," the voice repeated. *"Everyone will like a funny tap dance."*

I heard kids mumble and utter cries of surprise as I leaped up the steps at the side of the stage. Mayor Springfield hadn't seen me yet. He continued muttering into the microphone, something about how the legislature decides which new laws to consider.

Mr. Harkness had left the stage. I shielded my eyes as I stepped into the pool of bright stage lights. I could see the kids in the front rows . . . see their eyes grow wide in surprise.

And then there I was, beside the podium, two feet from the mayor. He finally looked up from his speech and saw me. There I was, and I started to dance. A crazy tap dance, swinging my arms up and down.

Tap tap. Taptaptap. Tappity tap tap.

The mayor made a choking sound, and his eyes nearly bulged out of his head.

Taptaptap. Tap tap. Taptaptaptap.

I swung my arms higher, leaning forward and tapping my heart out. I had a huge grin on my face. I knew I shouldn't be grinning, but I couldn't stop.

The mayor's speech slid off the podium and hit the floor. The pages scattered over the stage. I stepped to the side and began dancing on them.

"Crow like a rooster," the voice ordered. *"Keep dancing and crow to the ceiling."*

I tilted my head back, took a deep breath, and began to crow. The sound rang off the walls and rose over the screams and roars of everyone's laughter.

Several kids jumped to their feet and clapped along to the sounds of my tap-dancing. Kids shouted, "Go! Go! Go, Sammy. Go!" Others sat in horrified silence.

Mayor Springfield's mouth hung open. He kept blinking rapidly, as if he were trying to erase me from his eyes. He took a few stumbling steps backward, retreating from the podium.

I crowed again and again. I realized my crows were getting weaker. I was out of breath from all the crazy tapping. My chest started to ache.

Then I heard another command from the voice inside my head: *"Grab the mayor's hands and make him dance with you."*

I didn't hesitate. I couldn't resist the command. I was in the zone. I knew I had to do whatever the voice told me.

I tapped my way up to the mayor. I grabbed his hands and squeezed them in mine. His hands were wet and ice-cold. He was too startled to pull free.

I held his hands and began to spin him around in a circle. I spun him hard and made him move his feet. His face turned an angry red. He scowled and began uttering low grunts as he struggled to free himself. But I held on tight, swung his arms around, and kept dancing.

The auditorium rang with screams and wild roars of laughter. I could see teachers rushing to the stage from the back of the auditorium.

I stopped and started to spin the mayor in the opposite direction. Out of the corner of my eye, I saw Mr. Harkness stomping across the stage toward me. He was followed by the Gym teacher and his assistant.

"Get him *off* me!" Mayor Springfield yelled to them.

Mr. Harkness looked more stunned than angry. "Sammy—stop!" he shouted.

I kept dancing. The mayor broke free, but I

kept my shoes pounding the stage floor and started to swing my arms up and down again.

Mr. Boyle, the Gym teacher, grabbed me by the shoulders. Andrew, his assistant, tackled me around the waist. They pulled me to the floor on my back. But I kept my feet moving, kept dancing . . . until Andrew sat on my chest and Mr. Boyle pressed my feet to the floor with both hands.

I finally stopped. My muscles all went soft. My whole body slumped. A long *whoosh* escaped my mouth, like a balloon deflating. I began panting hard, unable to catch my breath.

A hush had fallen over the auditorium.

Principal Harkness leaned over me. His froggy eyes stared into mine. He lowered his face close to mine. "Sammy?" he asked. "Are you finished?"

"I don't know," I said.

26

Believe it or not, Mr. Harkness gave me one more chance.

We went to his office after the assembly, and he said since I've always been such a perfect student, he could forgive one crazy act. "After all, you weren't being vicious or dangerous," he said. "You were just having some fun—right?"

"Right," I said. "Fun."

I couldn't tell him why I ran up onstage and acted like a crazy lunatic. Mr. Harkness would never believe me. Or else he would think I had gone totally mental. He would send me home and tell my parents to get me to a head doctor as fast as possible.

Luckily, I didn't have to think of an excuse or a reason for my behavior. Mr. Harkness didn't even ask me why I did it.

"I know it was a dull assembly," Mr. Harkness said. "Springfield is the worst speaker I've ever seen. So I don't blame you for letting off a little steam." The principal chuckled. "Did you see the look on his face when you made him dance with you?"

Before that moment, I never realized that Mr. Harkness had a sense of humor. A lot of us make fun of him because his bald head and bulgy eyes make him look so much like a frog. But I realized he was a pretty good guy.

He told me I could go to lunch. "But no more stunts, Sammy. Do you hear me? I expect you to be the perfect student you've always been."

"Thank you, sir," I said, lowering my head. I couldn't believe he was letting me off so easy.

"One more stunt and I'll have to send you home and bring in your parents," he said.

"No problem," I murmured. And I was out the door and racing to the lunchroom.

I had to find Buzzy. I had to tell him about the voice, about why I was suddenly acting so crazy and weird. I knew Buzzy was the only one who would believe me.

He couldn't help me. But at least I'd have somebody on my side, somebody to talk to about the whole thing. Somebody who might under-stand what I was going through.

I stepped into the lunchroom and the kids all burst into applause. "Hey, Sammy—dance!" someone shouted. Everyone roared.

"Sammy—*you* should be mayor!"

"Go, Sammy!"

"Are you going to dance in class this afternoon?"

I gazed around the crowded room for Buzzy, but I didn't see him. My eyes stopped on the big tub of spaghetti, piled high with plenty of meatballs and tomato sauce, on the food counter.

My stomach growled. I suddenly realized I was hungry. The spaghetti looked pretty good.

"Hey, Sammy." Someone grabbed my arm. I turned and saw that it was Summer Magee. She flashed me two thumbs up. "Sammy, you were hilarious. I never laughed so hard in my life. You were wonderful."

Her amazing blue eyes gleamed under the bright lunchroom lights. Her smile made the two dimples appear on her cheeks.

"Uh . . . well . . . thanks," I managed to say.

"Go get your lunch," Summer said. "Then will you come sit with me at my table?"

Huh? Sit at her table? Sit at the table with all the hot, popular girls in school?

Was she serious?

I was about to say yes when I saw Buzzy walk into the lunchroom. "Uh . . . maybe tomorrow?" I told her. "I have something really important to tell Buzzy."

Her smile faded. And the glow faded from her eyes. "Okay. Tomorrow. Promise?"

"Promise," I said.

I walked over to Buzzy. He squinted at me. "Hey, what happened to you this morning?"

"That's what I want to talk to you about," I said. I started to pull him over to a table against the wall. But I suddenly heard the boy's voice again, so clearly, so insistent, in my ears:

"Do a cartwheel into the spaghetti pan."

I froze. I hoped I hadn't heard it correctly.

I saw Rubin Rubino enter the room. As he walked toward me, he gave me a two-fingered salute, tapping his fingers on his forehead. "Good work this morning, Sammy!" he called. "You looked like a jerk, but it was very funny."

"Do a cartwheel into the spaghetti pan," the voice repeated, a little louder.

I blinked.

"Sammy? Is something wrong?" Buzzy demanded.

"No. Just stand back," I said. I shoved him out of the way.

"Hey, what's up, Sammy?" Rubin said.

"Stand back," I warned. "Stand back." I lowered my head and took a running leap. I dipped my legs—sprang high—and did a cartwheel at the food counter.

WHUMMMP.

My shoes kicked the spaghetti pan and sent it flying. The noodles flew from the pan, a big red tomato-sauce glob. The pan crashed into the wall.

The huge ball of spaghetti came down fast—and splashed onto Rubin's head.

It made a surprisingly loud *splaaaat* sound. Spaghetti plopped over his hair and eyes. Meatballs rolled down his back. A thick river of tomato sauce oozed down the front of Rubin's T-shirt.

"Oops," I murmured.

Rubin grabbed the glob of spaghetti with both hands and frantically began to wipe it off his face and head. Noodles and meatballs went toppling to the floor.

"Rubin—"

I started to say it was an accident. But his name was the only word I got out—because, roaring like a ferocious animal, he came charging at me.

He wrapped his arms around my waist and tackled me to the floor.

I landed hard on my back, and he jumped on top of me. Grunting and growling, he swung his fists, landing punch after punch.

Eyes bulging, face dripping with tomato sauce, Rubin looked like a comic-book monster as he furiously sank his fists into my stomach.

Over my cries of pain, I heard the shrieks and horrified screams from the kids in the lunchroom. And then shadows rolled over Rubin and me. It took me a few seconds to realize the shadows were Miss Flake and two other teachers.

Rubin ignored them and kept swinging away, using me as a squealing punching bag. Finally, the three teachers dragged him off me. He was so crazed, he kept swinging his fists even after they stood him up against the wall.

I lay there on my back in a pool of spaghetti sauce, waiting for the pain to fade. I groaned as Mr. Harkness's froggy face suddenly appeared above me.

"That was your last chance, Sammy," he said. "I don't know what got into you. But you're out of here. I have to send you home."

I'm doomed, I realized. *My life is ruined.*

And that's when it started to get *really* dangerous.

27

Mr. Harkness phoned my parents at work. He asked them to come in for a talk about me later that afternoon.

Then he turned to me. I was hunched tensely in the chair in front of his desk, my hands tightly clasped in my lap. Spaghetti sauce smeared my shirt and jeans. "Sammy, can you explain what just happened in the lunchroom?"

I thought about it for a long moment. "Uh . . . not really," I said.

"You've been a perfect student," the principal said, rubbing his bald head. "Why did you suddenly decide to act funny and disturb everyone in school with your stunts?"

"I . . . don't really know," I answered. At first, I didn't want to tell him about the voice in my head that ordered me to do those things. I knew he wouldn't understand.

But sitting there in so much trouble, I suddenly

changed my mind. *I have to tell him. I have to make him believe me. Maybe he can help me.*

I took a deep breath and opened my mouth to start telling him the truth. And his office door swung open. Miss Pogue, his secretary, poked her head in. "Those school principals from downtown are waiting for you," she told Mr. Harkness.

He jumped to his feet. "Thank you, Miss Pogue." He turned back to me. "I'm sending you home. I'll talk to your parents when they arrive and decide what we should do about you, Sammy."

He motioned with both hands for me to leave. He shook his head sadly. "You're a mystery to me," he said.

Yes. Mystery is the right word, I thought.

I crept down the hall, pulled my backpack and jacket from my locker, and slumped out the front door of the school.

I took the long way home. I kept my head down, walking slowly, letting the wind gusts blow my coat behind me.

I walked past Marple House. Behind the tall hedges, the big house rose darkly, even though the afternoon sun was shining brightly now. I shuddered.

My problems with the voice started after that night in that old house. Did Marple House have something to do with my troubles? It seemed like a crazy idea.

I crossed the street onto Fairmont. Two squirrels stared at me from the tall grass in the empty lot on the corner. They stood stiffly, waiting for me to pass.

I was halfway down the block when the voice returned: *"Quick—climb that tree and rescue the kitten at the top."*

A shiver ran down my back. I wanted the voice to go away and never come back. But now it was telling me to climb a tree to do something nice?

I gazed up at the tall tree in front of me. The trunk was wide and smooth. Only a few leaves clung to the tangle of branches above my head. I looked hard for the kitten, but I couldn't see it from here.

"Quick," the voice repeated. *"Climb the tree. Rescue the kitten before it falls."*

I shivered again. I never climb trees. It's too dangerous. My parents said that *all* boys climb trees. But I never wanted to. I knew I'd fall and break my arm. I never understood why kids think tree climbing is fun.

"Quick!" the voice shouted.

The sharp sound made me jump. "No!" I started to protest. I tried to back away from the tree. I wanted to cross the street. Get as far from the tree as I could. I wanted to show the voice that *I* was in control.

But before I even realized it, I had my arms

wrapped around the cold, rough trunk. And I began to shinny up to the lower branches, tucking my legs around the trunk and hoisting myself up with my hands.

My heart was pounding like crazy when I reached the first limb.

Why am I doing this? I never climb trees.

The bark felt slippery and damp. It scratched my hands as I struggled to pull myself up. The wind picked up and lifted my coat behind me. My feet slipped. I grabbed the slender limb above me to keep from falling.

I steadied myself and gazed up to the thick limbs at the top of the tree. Where was the kitten? I still couldn't see it. "Hold tight—I'm coming!" I called to it.

Carefully, I hoisted myself onto the next branch. Then I crawled to the end of it and gripped the next higher branch and raised myself. My hands ached, scratched from the bark. My legs were trembling.

I kneeled on the branch and gazed around again. Clouds floated over the sun. The wind suddenly felt cooler. I shivered and stared at the top branches shifting in the breeze.

My muscles all tightened. "There's no kitten up here!" I shouted angrily.

The tree shook. A black SUV passed by without slowing. I peered down. The ground was far below. I'd climbed nearly to the top.

"Did you hear me?" I shouted. "There's no kitten up here."

Silence for a long moment. Then I heard laughter. Sharp, cold laughter. The voice didn't say a word. Just laughed that cruel laugh.

And as the laugh faded, the tree began to sway. My branch bobbed up and down. I wrapped my hands around it. And heard a loud *craaack*.

The branch tilted down sharply. I gasped and gripped it with all my strength. The branch was cracking, about to break.

I peered down again. *No way* I could climb down.

I heard another long *craaack*.

A wave of panic swept down my trembling body. And I began to scream. "Help me! Somebody! *Help me!*"

28

I didn't hear the sirens until I saw the fire truck squeal around the corner.

I scrambled to the trunk of the tree. The branch beneath my feet was about to snap off. It bounced beneath me. I wrapped my arms around the fat trunk and squeezed my body against it.

Was I strong enough to hold myself up if the branch cracked away and fell out from under me?

Luckily, I didn't have to find out. The firefighters had their ladder on the tree, and a grim-faced young guy with a black mustache and even blacker eyes reached for my arm. "Let go. Let go of the tree. It's okay," he said.

I didn't want to let go of the tree trunk. But he swung me around gently and, holding me tight, guided my legs to the ladder. He held on to me and we climbed down together.

When we stepped onto the ground, my legs were trembling so hard, I dropped onto my knees. A bunch of neighbors had gathered, and they all crowded around, asking if I was okay. A woman in a purple down coat pointed to the house across the street. "I live there. I saw you through the window. I called 911," she said.

I thanked her. I stood up, feeling steadier, calmer.

The firefighters were returning the ladder to their truck. "Why did you climb that tree?" the firefighter who rescued me asked.

I shrugged. "I . . . I thought there was a kitten up there."

He narrowed his eyes at me. "But the branches are bare. You can see all the way to the top. Couldn't you see there was no kitten?"

"I thought I saw one," I said.

"Dangerous," he murmured. He gazed up at the tree. "You should be careful, you know?"

"Thank you for saving my life," I said.

"Just be careful." He lowered his black fire-fighter helmet over his head, turned, and strode to the truck.

I took a deep breath and picked up my back-pack from the grass. People started to return to their houses. In a few minutes, I was standing there alone. My head was ringing. My legs were still shaky.

I didn't feel right. I felt angry. Angry and frightened.

I clenched my fists and I shouted, shouted to the voice inside my head. "What are you trying to do? *Kill* me?"

Silence.

And then the voice spoke up. And its words sent chill after chill down my back.

"You HAVE to die, Sammy. Then we can REALLY have fun."

PART FOUR

29

"Who are you?" I cried. "Why did you make me do those crazy things? Why do you want to kill me? Are you from Marple House?" The questions spilled from my mouth in a high, shrill voice.

"Haven't we had fun?" the voice said.

"Answer my questions," I said. "It hasn't been fun. It's been nothing but trouble for me."

A small red car filled with teenagers rolled past. Some of them gazed out the window at me. I wondered if they could see me talking to myself.

"Think of all the fun we can have together ..." the boy said, *"... when YOU'RE dead, too."*

I gasped. "So ... you *are* a ghost. From Marple House?"

And the memory came rushing back to me. Sitting in the dark, abandoned house ... watching the ghost-hunting gear ... watching and listening. And the sudden cold that invaded my body. The icy shock that froze me, froze my brain. The heavy cold that made me feel as if I were suddenly buried under an avalanche of snow.

That must have been the ghost.

"You . . . you invaded my mind?" I stammered.

"Yes, I did," he said. *"And we've been having such a good time. Wasn't it a great idea?"*

"No," I snapped. "Not a great idea. Why did you do it? Why did you invade my brain?"

"Because I'm so lonely," came the reply. *"Don't you know how lonely it is being a ghost? All those years by myself. No one to talk with. No one to laugh with."*

"And that's why you made me do those crazy things in school? That's why you ruined my life?" I demanded.

I saw a woman staring at me from a window in the house on the corner. She must have wondered why I was still standing there. I forced myself to start walking toward home.

"You have to leave me alone. Stop haunting me. Go home. Go haunt Marple House," I shouted.

"Haunting an empty old house is dreary. Boring," he said, sighing. *"Sammy, now you and I can both have fun together. We'll be best friends because we'll ALWAYS be together. And we'll have such a good time."*

"You—you mean when I'm *dead*?" I cried. "When I'm a ghost, too?"

Silence.

"Answer me!" I cried. "Do you really want me to be a ghost?"

Silence.

He didn't answer me. He had vanished.

But I didn't have to wait long for an answer.

The next day, the ghost killed me.

30

I ran the rest of the way home. I was desperate to talk to Mom and Dad. I had to tell them I was haunted.

I didn't know how they could help me with this problem. But they had to know. They had to believe me and understand why I'd been acting so differently.

How do you get rid of a ghost who has decided he wants to be your best friend forever?

Maybe my parents knew of a doctor or some kind of scientist who could help with the problem.

The house was empty. My parents were at school, talking with Principal Harkness. Getting the bad news. I knew they wouldn't be in good moods when they returned home. But I would explain everything to them. They had to believe me now. They had to help me.

I waited for them in the living room, tensely pacing back and forth, my brain spinning. When

152

my dad's grandfather clock began to chime five o'clock, it startled me so much, I nearly jumped out of my skin.

Mom and Dad burst in a few minutes later. I hurried to greet them.

"Mr. Harkness said you can come back to school tomorrow," Mom said before I had a chance to even say hello.

"We need to have a long discussion," Dad said.

"Yes, we do," I said breathlessly. "You see—"

"But not now." He cut me off. "Your mom and I are going to be late for our Elks banquet. We're on the committee, and we're supposed to get there early."

Mom shook her head. "I wanted to change my dress. But I guess I'll have to go in this."

"You look fine," Dad said.

"No, I don't," Mom fretted. "You just don't want me to spend time getting changed. And I didn't get to do my hair. I wanted to look nice tonight, but—"

I lost it. "YOU HAVE TO LISTEN TO ME!" I screamed.

Dad spun to face me. "No, we don't, Sammy," he said sharply. "We've heard enough about you for one day. We'll discuss everything tomorrow. But *we'll* be doing the talking—not you."

I knew they'd be angry. I didn't blame them. But I had to make them listen to me.

"I have a ghost in my head," I started.

153

Mom hurried out of the room. Dad was already out the front door. "I'll wait for you in the car," he shouted to Mom.

"I have to tell you about the ghost," I said when Mom returned.

"Your dinner is in the fridge," she said, rushing past me, brushing down her hair with both hands. "Mrs. O'Connor will look in on you later."

She hurried out of the room and slammed the front door behind her. A few seconds later, I watched them back down the driveway and disappear.

And there I was . . . all alone. Except for a ghost who planned to kill me.

The next morning, I overslept. Dad had already left for work. Mom was hurrying out the door. "Have some cereal for breakfast," she said. "And listen, Sammy—no more reports from school, okay?"

She was out the door before I could answer.

Mr. Harkness was giving me one more chance. But I didn't want to go to school. I was afraid of what the ghost might order me to do. I wanted to stay in my room and hide and be safe.

Then I thought, maybe I'd be safer in school. Around people. In case I needed help.

It was a cold November day. It had snowed a little the night before, less than an inch, but there were patches of snow on the lawns. The sky was charcoal gray, threatening more.

I crossed the street to the school, when Summer Magee came running up to me. "Hey, Sammy." She punched my shoulder like we were old pals. "Good job yesterday."

I turned to her in surprise. "Excuse me? Good job?"

She grinned. "Dumping the spaghetti on Rubin? Awesome!"

I groaned. "It got me kicked out of school."

"Worth it," Summer said. "Misty got the whole thing on video. She just happened to have her phone out. Want me to message it to you?"

"Uh . . . No thanks."

The spaghetti video had probably gone viral. That meant Rubin was already planning his revenge. Pain time for me. But, of course, I now had bigger worries than Rubin Rubino.

As we started up the walk to the front entrance, Summer seemed happy to walk with me. This was a major change, and I hoped I would live long enough to enjoy it.

But a few feet from the front doors, the voice in my head returned with a new order—the most dangerous and crazy command yet.

31

"So are you going to do something crazy today?" Summer asked.

I shook my head. "Not today. I think I'll take it easy today. You know. Give Miss Flake a break."

She made a pouty face. "But school is so much more exciting when you do something totally nutty."

"*Too* exciting," I muttered. We stepped up to the front entrance.

And I heard the boy's voice clearly in my head: *"Climb up on the roof and show off your dance moves."*

I gasped. "But I don't have any dance moves," I cried.

Summer stared at me. "Sammy? I didn't ask you to dance with me."

"I know," I said. "I—"

"Get up there and start dancing," the voice ordered.

"But I don't want to climb up on the roof!" I shouted.

Summer squinted at me. "Climb up on the roof? What are you *talking* about? I didn't say a word about the roof."

I couldn't explain to her. I gazed up at the roof. I gritted my teeth, struggling to resist the ghost's command. *I won't do it. I won't do it*, I repeated to myself.

Then I spotted a drainpipe on the side of the front door. Before I realized it, I was scrambling up to the slanted tile roof. The roof tilted down sharply. It was hard to balance. But I stepped to the edge and began to dance.

My feet scraped the tiles. I swung my arms around, humming a tune to myself to dance to.

"Sammy—get down!" I heard Summer cry from down below. "You'll *kill* yourself."

"Faster!" the ghost demanded. *"Dance faster!"*

I had no choice. I began to pick up speed. Bending my knees, tapping my sneakers on the tile roof, shooting my arms from side to side.

I heard laughter. And screams.

I glanced down and saw that a small crowd had gathered. Some of them began to cheer: "Go, Sammy! Go, Sammy! Go, Sammy!"

I saw that Summer was grinning and clapping along with them.

"Don't you realize he's trying to *kill* me?" I shouted to the crowd.

But they were cheering and chanting and laughing so loudly, they couldn't hear me.

My feet slapped the roof. My heart pounded in a crazy rhythm in my chest. I shot my arms up and down and bobbed my head in time to the silent song in my head.

"Dance! Dance! Dance!" some kids screamed.

"Faster! Dance faster!" the ghost demanded.

I was panting now, struggling to breathe. My knees bending, my shoes slapping the edge of the tiles.

And that's when I fell.

My sneakers slipped on the tiles and I toppled forward. I shoved both arms out as if I could stop my fall.

But no. I was toppling headfirst off the roof. Flapping my arms like a frantic bird and kicking my feet as I dropped.

I'm going to die now, I told myself. *The ghost is getting his wish.*

32

I landed on my head. Pain roared through my body. My arms and legs flopped over the hard ground. I didn't move. I knew I was dead.

And then . . . I blinked my eyes and raised my head and struggled to focus. And slowly realized I hadn't landed on the ground.

I'd landed on Mr. Harkness.

He was sprawled on his back on the grass, his mouth open, eyes dazed. It took a few seconds to figure out that I'd landed on top of him. And now I was lying across his chest. Blinking and forcing myself to breathe and staring up at the crowd of kids and teachers who had formed a circle around us.

Mr. Harkness croaked, a long, loud groan. His eyes still spun crazily. I saw grass stains on the top of his bald head. He moved one arm awkwardly. I think he was trying to shove me off him.

"Sammy, can you get up?" he rasped weakly.

"I don't know," I answered. I forced myself to a sitting position on top of his chest. His shirt had ripped open, and his gray, striped necktie was tight around his neck.

With a groan, I pulled myself to my feet. My legs were trembling so hard, I thought I might fall again.

Mr. Harkness still didn't move. He stared up at me. "Strike three," he said. "Do you hear what I'm saying, Sammy?"

"I'm out?"

He nodded. "For the second time. Strike three for the second time. Go home. I'll phone your parents. I'm sure they can find you another school. And maybe they'll get you some dance lessons . . . since you like to dance so much."

I lowered my head. My legs were still trembling as I started to walk toward the street. I saw Summer Magee wave at me and flash me a thumbs-up. I saw Mr. Boyle and his assistant struggle to pull Mr. Harkness to his feet.

I shoved my hands deep into my pockets as I walked. I took several deep breaths. The ghost had tried to kill me. He seriously wanted me dead.

My mind did flip-flops as I slowly walked away from the school. I had to find a way to get the ghost out of my head. No one else would believe me. No one else would help me.

Suddenly, I knew what I had to do. It was crazy. And desperate. But I had no choice. I turned at the corner and began walking faster, on my way to Marple House.

33

Even though the morning sun was high in the sky, the big, old house lay covered in shadow. I shuddered as I trudged up through the tall grass and weeds on the front lawn.

Ignoring my thudding heartbeats, I found the window at the end of the house where my friends and I had broken in. I hoisted myself onto the stone ledge, then eased myself carefully into the house.

I took a few steps, hugging myself. It was at least ten degrees colder in here than outside. Shafts of sunlight through the dirt-smeared windows cast long, eerie shadows across the bare floorboards.

My shoes scraped loudly as I made my way down the long back hall toward the room where we had set up our ghost-hunting equipment.

I was nearly there when I heard a startled cry. *"Hey, I died in this house,"* the voice said. *"Why did you bring me back here?"*

"I brought you back home," I said. "This is where you belong."

"*No!*" he protested. "*You're going to join me, remember? We're going to haunt everyone together. We're going to be best friends—forever!*"

"No way," I said. "Get out. Get out of my head. I don't want to die. I don't want to be a ghost."

"*Sammy, it won't hurt*," he insisted. "*I promise. It will be the BEST!*"

"No!" I said. But I felt myself being pulled forward. I saw a narrow door cut into the back wall. The door was black and the doorknob was black, and the hall grew darker and darker as I moved toward it.

"*It's a special place. The door between life and death*," the voice whispered.

"No! Please!" I screamed. A dark mist seeped from under the door and washed over me, a heavy, smothering fog.

I tried to pull back. I tried to turn away. But the force of the ghost was too powerful.

"Nooooo!" I uttered one more scream as the black door swung open, and I was flung through it, pushed hard—into the deepest blackness I had ever seen.

Deep, endless blackness, and a shuddering cold. I fell through the inky blackness, through clouds of blackness. Until all was silent and still, and I knew I didn't exist anymore. I was part of the darkness. I was gone.

34

Were my eyes open or closed? The darkness was so heavy, I couldn't tell. But then a pale light seeped down from above me. Slowly, the hallway came back into focus.

As my eyes adjusted to the brightness, I saw that I was not alone. A boy about my age stood next to me, watching me intently. He had long brown hair and dark, serious eyes. His face was as white as flour.

His clothes were heavy and old-fashioned, a dress shirt that buttoned to the neck, flannel suit trousers, and big black leather shoes.

"Wh-who are you?" I stammered.

"I'm Benjamin Marple," he said, the dark eyes still studying me. "I'm the one who haunted you."

"B-but I can *see* you!" I cried.

"That's because you're like me now," he said.

I sucked in a breath. "You mean . . . I'm dead?"

"Don't think about it, Sammy," he said. "Follow me. Let's have some fun. You'll see. You'll like being a ghost." He turned and began to float down the hallway toward the front of the house.

I gasped as I realized I was floating, too. My shoes were at least a foot above the floor!

We floated right through the front wall and out to the street. "Benjamin, where are we going?" I called.

He didn't look back. "Just follow me, Sammy. I'm going to show you how much fun this can be."

Two cars came down the street. We floated right over them. We sailed past four workers cutting limbs off a tree. They didn't turn around. I realized they couldn't see us. We were invisible.

"Benjamin, wait!" I called as my school came into view.

"We don't want to waste time, Sammy," he replied. "I know you're going to like this."

I tried to stop at the front of the school building. But Benjamin grabbed me by the hand—and pulled me right through the wall.

This can't be happening. That was my thought as we floated through the front hall, past the principal's office, moving toward Miss Flake's classroom. But, of course, it *was* happening.

No one turned as we entered the room through the chalkboard. No one stared or cried out in shock. They couldn't see me or Benjamin. We were dead and invisible.

And then Benjamin pulled me down the row of

desks until we were in front of Rubin Rubino. Rubin had his head down, his dark hair falling over his face. He was doodling on his yellow notepad, drawing some kind of rocket car.

"Follow me," Benjamin whispered. He took my hand again. And we both leaped off the floor *and into Rubin's head.*

"I—I—I—" I sputtered. I didn't know what to say. I didn't know what Benjamin planned to do here. But I knew. I definitely knew we were inside Rubin Rubino's brain.

"Watch," Benjamin whispered. "Watch this, Sammy. This is going to be very funny. You will like this. I promise."

And then in a loud voice, he said to Rubin: "Stand up, Rubin. Walk to the front of the room. Call Miss Flake *Mommy.* Then suck your thumb like a baby."

From my spot in Rubin's brain, I could see everything perfectly.

Rubin hesitated. Then he slowly climbed to his feet. He strode down the aisle toward the front of the room till he reached Miss Flake's desk.

She looked up from the textbook she was reading. "Rubin?" she asked. "Is there a problem?"

He shook his head. "No, Mommy," he said. "No problem, Mommy." Then he curled his thumb into his mouth and began to suck it, making loud slurping noises.

Miss Flake gasped. The class went nuts, laughing, howling, shouting. Rubin stood there looking confused.

I laughed, too. "Hey, you're right," I told Benjamin. "This IS going to be fun!"

But . . . the fun lasted only one day.

35

We had an awesome time inside Rubin's brain. In Art class, we made him pull off his shirt and paint his chest blue. In Swim class, we made him do a belly flop into the pool with all his clothes on. Then when Rubin was dragged from the pool, we made him spit water right into the coach's face.

At lunch we forced him to stuff meatloaf into his armpits. Then we made him find Mr. Boyle and ordered him to rub his face into the Gym teacher's mashed potatoes.

I never laughed so hard when I was alive. What a beautiful revenge on Rubin for all the terror he had caused me.

I told Benjamin that the day was way fun. But when the afternoon bell rang and everyone started to go home, I suddenly felt sad. More than sad. I felt doomed.

Benjamin and I floated out of Rubin's brain and made our invisible way out of the school building. I saw Buzzy walking with Todd and Misty, heading for home. And I wanted to walk with them and talk to them.

But I would never be able to talk to them again.

I followed them for a while, floating above the street and front yards. When my house came into view, I totally lost it. A sob escaped my throat.

I missed my mom and dad. I missed my home.

Sure, it was awesome to make Rubin act crazy, to get him in the worst trouble of his life. It was terrific fun.

But being alive was a lot more fun.

I turned to Benjamin. "What can I do?" I asked him. "I want to be alive again. Tell me. Is there any way I can reverse what happened to me?"

He narrowed his dark eyes and a sneer crossed his face. "Of course not," he said.

36

I didn't believe him. I knew he would lie to keep me a ghost, to keep me with him. But I had a plan. I knew what I had to do.

It meant going back to Marple House. Back to the black door at the end of the hallway.

Benjamin tried to stop me. "Stop! Hey—where are you going, Sammy?"

I flew away from him. I knew he was chasing after me. I moved as fast as I could, back into the creepy old house. Down the hall, floating above the floor, so light and invisible.

Into the blackness that surrounded the narrow door at the back wall.

"Sammy—stop! Stop right there! Sammy—don't go there!"

Benjamin's cries were so frantic, I thought maybe my plan would work. Maybe if I went back through the door, back into that horrifying darkness . . . maybe I would come out alive again.

With a determined roar, I bolted to the far wall and grabbed the black doorknob. I started to twist it, to pull the door open—and felt Benjamin's strong hands on my shoulders.

"No!" he protested. "No—you can't!"

He jerked me back, pulled me away from the door. Dragged me to the floor. I struggled to free myself. He sat on top of me and pressed my arms to the floor.

"You can't do it! You can't do it!" he shrieked.

We wrestled there in the deep shadow of the door. Finally, I struggled to my feet. He was clinging to my back. But I dove forward and heaved the door open—and burst through it.

Into the deep black . . . growing deeper . . . heavier . . . Like a black ocean wave rising high and sweeping over me in all its icy horror.

The darkness swirled around me faster and faster. I couldn't see or breathe or move. I didn't exist. I was a part of the darkness. Only darkness.

Oh, no, I thought. *Oh, no. This isn't working. This isn't working at all.*

37

And then I saw a dim yellow light.

The light spread and brightened until I could see clearly again. Trembling, I realized I was staring into sunlight from the window at the front of the hall.

I started trotting toward it. My sneakers clumped on the floor. I tried to float. I couldn't. I brushed my hand along the wall. I could feel it. My hand couldn't go through the wall.

I'm real again.

I pushed open the front door and jumped down the stairs. I did a cartwheel across the tall grass. "I'm alive!" I screamed. "Alive! Alive again!"

I raised my face and shouted at the sun, a shout of total joy.

I was me. Sammy Baker. Alive.

"Benjamin?" I spun in a full circle. No sign of him out here. I stared into the dark front windows of the house. "Benjamin?"

No. He was gone.

I did another cartwheel. I felt *amazing*.

I ran all the way home. "Mom! Dad! I'm so happy to see you! I ... I missed you so much!" I screamed. I hugged them both, squeezing them tight.

They looked at one another. "Sammy, what's gotten into you?" Dad asked. "We're happy to see you, too. But don't act crazy. We saw you this morning, remember?"

Mom studied me. "Let me feel your forehead. Are you sick?"

"No. Just happy," I said.

I felt like doing another cartwheel. It was so good to be home and be alive.

The next morning, I couldn't wait to get to school. Mom and Dad had fixed everything up with Mr. Harkness. Believe it or not, he was giving me one more chance.

I took my seat and gazed around, so glad to see my friends again.

Miss Flake entered the room, followed by a boy in dark clothes, who stood half-hidden behind her. "We have a new student, everyone," she announced. "This is Benjamin Marple. Please make him feel welcome."

I gasped. Benjamin? Yes. Benjamin.

"You can take the empty desk next to Sammy," Miss Flake told him, pointing.

My heart started to pound. Benjamin? But . . . everyone could see him. Was he . . . alive?

He sank into the seat next to me and leaned close. "Happy to see me, Sammy?" he whispered.

"H-how?" I stammered. "You're not a ghost? You're alive?"

He nodded. "I held on to you as you went through the door. I think that's why it worked. I've tried to return to the living on my own, but I guess I've been dead too long. I needed someone else to pull me through. And you were the one. I'm alive again, thanks to you."

I didn't know what to say. I just stared at him with my mouth hanging open.

Benjamin's dark eyes flashed. "We're going to have a lot of fun, Sammy," he said.

I swallowed. "Fun? What kind of fun?"

"Don't worry. I'll show you."

At lunch, he pulled me outside. "Okay, let's go," he said. "Up on the roof. Let's show off our best dance moves."

"No way!" I cried. "No way!"

I watched him shinny up the drainpipe and pull himself onto the roof.

"No way! I mean it. No way." I said.

But my hands were gripping the drainpipe. What was happening? Why was I pulling myself hand-over-hand up to the dangerous, slanting roof?

"No way!" I repeated. "Benjamin—no way!"

Benjamin laughed. "We came through the tunnel together, Sammy. We're connected *forever*."

So here I am, standing on the roof. Here I am. And here I go, about to show off my best dance moves.

A crowd has gathered. Summer Magee is smiling at me from down below.

What could go wrong?

HERE COMES
THE SHAGGEDY

Here's a sneak peek!

The swamp at night makes trickling sounds, gurgling, popping. The river water is alive, and the sand shifts and moves as if it's restless. The chitter and whistle of insects never stops. Birds flap in the bending tree limbs, and red-eyed bats flutter low, dipping into the water for a fast drink, then soaring to meet the darkness.

The eerie sounds made Becka Munroe's skin tingle. She sat alert in the slender rowboat, every muscle in her body tensed and tight. She kept her eyes on the dark shoreline. Her hands on the oars felt cold and wet.

"Donny, you're crazy," she said, her voice muffled in the steamy night air. "I don't like this. We shouldn't be here."

"They won't miss their stupid rowboat," her boyfriend, Donny Albert, said. His oars splashed water, then hit sand. The river was shallow enough here for their boat to get stuck. "We'll leave it for them up on the shore."

"I'm not talking about stealing this boat," Becka said, fighting the shivers that rolled down her back despite the heat of the night. "Why are we here? Why are we on the river at night in this frightening swamp? I . . . I can't see a thing. There isn't even a moon."

Donny snickered. "For thrills," he said. "Life is so boring, Becka. Tenth grade is so boring. Go to school. Do your homework. Sleep and go to school again. We have to do something crazy. Something exciting."

Becka sighed. "I can't believe I agreed to come out here at night. Why did I do it?"

She could see his grin even in the dim light. "Because you're crazy about me?"

"Just plain crazy," she muttered.

Something splashed up from the water and thumped the side of the boat. "Did you hear that?" Becka cried. "What was it? A frog?"

"Snake, maybe," Donny said. "The river is crawling with them. Some are a mile long."

"Shut up!" Becka snapped. She had a sudden urge to take an oar and swing it at Donny's head. "You're not funny. It's scary enough out here without you trying to scare me more."

He laughed. "You're too easy to scare. It's not much of a challenge. I don't think —"

He didn't finish his sentence. His mouth remained open and his dark eyes bulged. He was staring past Becka. His chin began to quiver and a low moan escaped his throat. He raised a finger and pointed.

Becka heard the splash of water behind her. And the heavy *slap* of footsteps on wet sand. "Donny — what?" she uttered. Then she turned and saw the huge creature.

It took her eyes a few seconds to focus. At first, she thought she was staring at a tall swamp bush, some kind of piney shrub looming up from the sandy bottom.

But as soon as she realized it was moving in the water, taking long, wet, splashing strides ... she knew it was alive. Knew it was a terrifying creature.

"Row! Hurry! Row!" Donny's scream came out high and shrill. He bent over the oars and began to pull frantically. She could hear his wheezing breaths. But they were quickly drowned out by the grunts of the swamp monster that staggered toward them and its thudding, wet footsteps.

The creature stood at least ten feet tall. It was shaped like a human but covered in dark fur like a bear. Chunks of wet sand fell off its fur as it staggered forward. It raised its curled claws and uttered an angry howl of attack.

"Oh, help. Oh, help." One oar slipped out of Becka's hand. She grabbed at it and caught it before it dropped into the water. Then she leaned forward and began to row as hard as she could.

About the Author

R.L. Stine's books are read all over the world. So far, his books have sold more than 300 million copies, making him one of the most popular children's authors in history. Besides Goosebumps, R.L. Stine has written the teen series Fear Street and the funny series Rotten School, as well as the Mostly Ghostly series, The Nightmare Room series, and the two-book thriller *Dangerous Girls*. R.L. Stine lives in New York with his wife, Jane, and Minnie, his King Charles spaniel. You can learn more about him at www.RLStine.com.

NOW A MAJOR MOTION PICTURE

JACK BLACK

Goosebumps

The Original Bone-Chilling Series

—with Exclusive
Author Interviews!

NIGHT of the LIVING DUMMY
R.L. STINE

DEEP TROUBLE
R.L. STINE

MONSTER BLOOD
R.L. STINE

the HAUNTED MASK
R.L. STINE

ONE DAY at HORRORLAND
R.L. STINE

the CURSE of the MUMMY'S TOMB
R.L. STINE

BE CAREFUL WHAT YOU WISH FOR
R.L. STINE

SAY CHEESE and DIE!
R.L. STINE

the HORROR at CAMP JELLYJAM
R.L. STINE

HOW I GOT MY SHRUNKEN HEAD
R.L. STINE

SCHOLASTIC

www.scholastic.com/goosebumps

GBCL22

R. L. Stine's Fright Fest!
Now with Splat Stats and More!

Goosebumps
GHASTLY MISCHIEF AWAITS...
WWW.SCHOLASTIC.COM/GOOSEBUMPS
GET GHOUL-YARD GOSSIP!
EXPLORE EVERY BOOK!
PLAY THRILLING GAMES!
SAMPLE SPOOKY AUDIOBOOKS!
JOIN THE FAN FORUM!
WATCH MONSTROUS VIDEOS!

Catch the MOST WANTED Goosebumps® villains UNDEAD OR ALIVE!

WANTED
THE HAUNTED MASK
R.L. STINE

PLANET OF THE LAWN GNOMES
R.L. STINE

SON OF SLAPPY
R.L. STINE

HOW I MET MY MONSTER
R.L. STINE

FRANKENSTEIN'S DOG
R.L. STINE

DR. MANIAC WILL SEE YOU NOW
R.L. STINE

CREATURE TEACHER: THE FINAL EXAM
R.L. STINE

A NIGHTMARE ON CLOWN STREET
R.L. STINE

NIGHT OF THE PUPPET PEOPLE
R.L. STINE

HERE COMES THE SHAGGEDY
R.L. STINE

ZOMBIE HALLOWEEN
R.L. STINE

THE 12 SCREAMS OF CHRISTMAS
R.L. STINE

TRICK OR TRAP
R.L. STINE

SPECIAL EDITIONS

■SCHOLASTIC
scholastic.com/goosebumps

GBMW10